A Book of

INDUSTRIAL PHARMACY - II

For T. Y. B. Pharm
Semester VI

As Per the Syllabus

Mrs. Trusha P. Shangrapawar
M. Pharm. (Pharmaceutics)
Assistant Professor
PDEA's Shankarrao Ursal College of
Pharmaceutical Sciences and Research Centre
Kharadi, Pune 14.

Mr. Sujit S. Kakade
M. Pharm. (Pharmaceutics)
Assistant Professor
PDEA's Shankarrao Ursal College of
Pharmaceutical Sciences and Research Centre
Kharadi, Pune 14.

Mr. Prashant H. Khade
M. Pharm. (Pharmaceutics)
Assistant Professor
PDEA's Shankarrao Ursal College of
Pharmaceutical Sciences and Research Centre
Kharadi, Pune 14.

NIRALI PRAKASHAN
ADVANCEMENT OF KNOWLEDGE

N1723

Industrial Pharmacy - II ISBN 978-93-86353-34-4

First Edition : January 2017

© : Authors

Published By :   POD

NIRALI PRAKASHAN

Abhyudaya Pragati, 1312, Shivaji Nagar,
Off J.M. Road, PUNE – 411005
Tel - (020) 25512336/37/39, Fax - (020) 25511379
Email : niralipune@pragationline.com

☞ DISTRIBUTION CENTRES

PUNE

Nirali Prakashan : 119, Budhwar Peth, Jogeshwari Mandir Lane, Pune 411002, Maharashtra
Tel : (020) 2445 2044, 66022708, Fax : (020) 2445 1538
Email : bookorder@pragationline.com, niralilocal@pragationline.com

Nirali Prakashan : S. No. 28/27, Dhyari, Near Pari Company, Pune 411041
Tel : (020) 24690204 Fax : (020) 24690316
Email : dhyari@pragationline.com, bookorder@pragationline.com

MUMBAI

Nirali Prakashan : 385, S.V.P. Road, Rasdhara Co-op. Hsg. Society Ltd.,
Girgaum, Mumbai 400004, Maharashtra
Tel : (022) 2385 6339 / 2386 9976, Fax : (022) 2386 9976
Email : niralimumbai@pragationline.com

☞ DISTRIBUTION BRANCHES

JALGAON

Nirali Prakashan : 34, V. V. Golani Market, Navi Peth, Jalgaon 425001,
Maharashtra, Tel : (0257) 222 0395, Mob : 94234 91860

KOLHAPUR

Nirali Prakashan : New Mahadvar Road, Kedar Plaza, 1st Floor Opp. IDBI Bank
Kolhapur 416 012, Maharashtra. Mob : 9850046155

NAGPUR

Pratibha Book Distributors :Above Maratha Mandir, Shop No. 3, First Floor,
Rani Jhanshi Square, Sitabuldi, Nagpur 440012, Maharashtra
Tel : (0712) 254 7129

DELHI

Nirali Prakashan : 4593/21, Basement, Aggarwal Lane 15, Ansari Road, Daryaganj
Near Times of India Building, New Delhi 110002
Mob : 08505972553

BENGALURU

Pragati Book House : House No. 1, Sanjeevappa Lane, Avenue Road Cross,
Opp. Rice Church, Bengaluru – 560002.
Tel : (080) 64513344, 64513355,Mob : 9880582331, 9845021552
Email:bharatsavla@yahoo.com

CHENNAI

Pragati Books : 9/1, Montieth Road, Behind Taas Mahal, Egmore,
Chennai 600008 Tamil Nadu, Tel : (044) 6518 3535,
Mob : 94440 01782 / 98450 21552 / 98805 82331,
Email : bharatsavla@yahoo.com

niralipune@pragationline.com | www.pragationline.com

Also find us on f www.facebook.com/niralibooks

Acknowledgement ...

We take this opportunity to express sincere gratitude to our parents and family members for providing their moral support and enabling us to utilize the crucial spare time for successive completion of this book.

We would like to thanks Hon. Shri. Ajitdada Pawar, President, Pune District Education Association, Shri. Sandip Kadam, Secretary, Pune District Education Association, Shri. Rajendra Ghadge, President Representative, Pune District Education Association and Shri. A. M. Jadhav, Joint Secretary (Administration), Pune District Education Association.

We are thankful to our Principal, Teaching Staff, Non-teaching staff and students of PDEA's Shankarrao Ursal College of Pharmacy, Kharadi, Pune, for encouraging us to venture into writing this book.

We are grateful to the publishers, Mr. Dineshbhai Furia and Mr. Jignesh Furia of Nirali Prakashan for providing us with the opportunity to write this book. We appreciate the co-operation from Mr. Ilyas Shaikh for the excellent DTP work, Mrs. Manasi Pingle for proof reading the text, Miss Shilpa Zade for the figures, Mr. Ravindra Walodare for the cover and the entire staff of Nirali Prakashan, especially Dr. S. B. Gokhale and Mr. Nitin Thorat in bringing out this book in the shortest time period.

Authors

Preface ...

We take pride in presenting this book of Industrial Pharmacy - II for the Third Year Pharmacy (Semester-VI) degree course as per revised syllabus. We have written this book in such a fashion whereby students can acquire the knowledge required for Third Year B. Pharmacy (Semester-VI).

This book contains five chapters and an attempt is made to provide point by point account of syllabus which has been meticulously arranged to make the overall studies easier and more enjoyable. The suitable figures have been included to give good illustration of text. A special efforts based upon previous university examination have been taken during the frameworks of each topic.

Every chapter includes a question bank containing probable questions along with questions from earlier university question papers to help students to prepare better in the examination.

We have made every attempt, strived hard to present a good book. We would appreciate any suggestions and criticism from the teachers and students for future improvement of this book.

Authors

Syllabus ...

1. Disperse Systems   4 Hrs.

Free energy consideration, Thermodynamic v/s kinetic stability, DLVO theory, Classification of disperse system

2. Suspensions   12 Hrs.

Flocculated and Deflocculated system Stokes law.

Formulation development, Excipients used in manufacturing of suspensions: Suspending agents, wetting agents, dispersants, deflocculating and flocculating agents, Structured vehicle, preservatives, colour, flavour.

Formulation of suspensions: Low solid content, high solid content, antacid suspension, suspensions for reconstitution.

Evaluation of suspensions: Rheology, particle size, volume of sedimentation and degree of sedimentation, particle charges and caking in suspensions, importance of changes in solubility because of changes in particle size, polymorphic form of temperature, labeling of suspensions.

3. Emulsions   12 Hrs.

Physicochemical principles, theory of emulsification, energy barriers to coalescence. Film barriers, steric stabilization.

Stability of emulsions: Creaming, coalescence, cracking, HLB value and phase inversion temperature, kraft point, cloud point.

Excipients used in emulsions: Emulsifier and choice of emulsifier, vehicles, preservatives, antioxidants, colour, flavour.

Formulation of emulsions, multiple emulsions, microemulsions.

Evaluation of emulsion

Emulsion stability, stress testing. Evaluation: Phase separation, pH, globule size, viscosity, redisperibility.

4. Semisolid Dosage Forms   12 Hrs.

Anatomy and physiology of skin (Introduction)

Types: ointment, cream, paste and gels.

Formulation development and manufacturing: Semisolid bases and additives, special reference to penetration enhancers, Selection criteria of bases. Percutaneous absorption: Flux and its measurement, factors affecting drugs. Properties, vehicle related and patient related.

Evaluation parameters: Globule particle size, pH, spreadability, permeation, drug release, viscosity, drug content, extrudability, skin irritation tests.

5. Manufacturing Equipments   5 Hrs.

Suspension, emulsion and semisolids. Layout and designing of manufacturing facility for suspension, emulsion and semisolids as per schedule M.

✍ ✍ ✍

Contents ...

Disperse Systems

Contents...

1.1 Introduction

A disperse system is defined as, "a heterogeneous, two-phase system in which the internal (dispersed, discontinuous) phase is distributed or dispersed within the continuous (external) phase or vehicle". Various pharmaceutical systems are included in this definition, the internal and external phases being gases, liquids or solids. Disperse systems are also important in other fields of application, e.g., processing and manufacturing of household and industrial products such as cosmetics, foods and paints.

1.2 Classification of Disperse System

(1) Classification based on the physical state of the two constituent phases :

The dispersed phase and the dispersion medium can be solids, liquids or gases. Pharmaceutically most important are suspensions, emulsions and aerosols. A suspension is solid/liquid dispersion, e.g., a solid drug is dispersed within a liquid that is a poor solvent for the drug. An emulsion is a liquid/liquid dispersion in which the two phases are completely immiscible or with each other. In the case of aerosols, either a liquid (e.g. drug solution) or a solid (e.g., fine drug particles) is dispersed within a gaseous phase. There is no disperse system in which both phases are gases.

Table 1.1: Classification based on the physical state of the two constituent phases

Dispersed phase	Dispersion medium		
	Solid	Liquid	Gas
Solid	Solid suspension (zinc oxide paste, tooth paste)	Suspension (tetracycline oral suspension USP, bentonite magma NF)	Solid aerosol (epinephrine bitartrate inhalation aerosol USP, smoke
Liquid	Solid emulsion (hydrophilic petrolatum USP, butter)	Emulsion (mineral oil emulsion USP, milk)	Liquid aerosol (nasal sprays, fog)
Gas	Solid foam Foamed plastics Pumice	Foam Effervescent salts in water Carborated beverages	None

(2) Based on the particle size of the dispersed phase: Dispersions are generally classified as molecular dispersions, colloidal dispersions, and coarse dispersions.

1. **Molecular dispersions:** Molecular dispersions have dispersed particles lower than 1 nm in size. E.g. Sugar solution.

2. **Colloidal dispersions:** Colloidal dispersions have particle sizes between 1 nm and 1000 nm. E.g. Microemulsions, nanoparticles, microspheres are some of the examples of colloidal dispersions.

3. **Coarse dispersions:** Coarse dispersions have particle size greater than 1000 nm, which includes suspensions and emulsions.

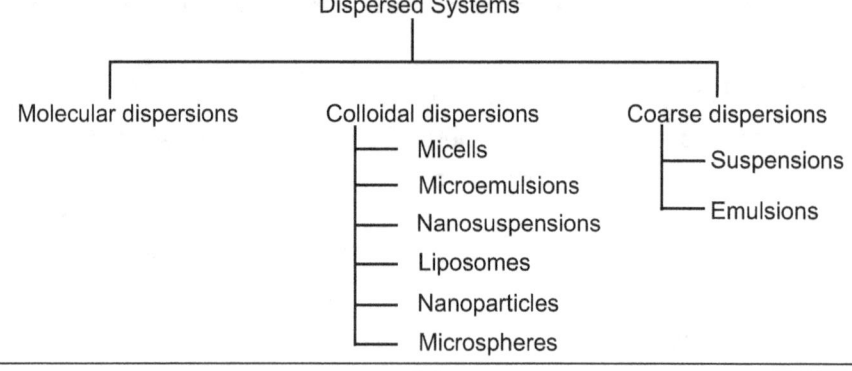

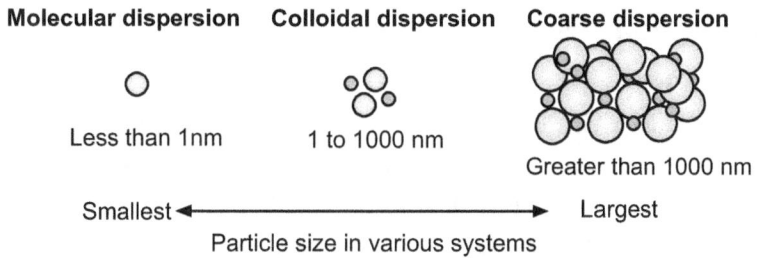

Fig. 1.1: Types of dispersion system

Table 1.2: Some important properties of molecular, colloidal and coarse dispersion

Sr. no.	Name of property	Molecular dispersion	Colloidal dispersion	Coarse dispersion
1.	Size	Size of particles is less than 1 nm.	Size of particles is between 1 nm and 1000 nm.	Size of particles is greater than 1000 nm.
2.	Filterability	Pass through ordinary filter paper and also through animal membrane.	Pass through ordinary filter paper but not through animal membrane.	Do not pass through filter paper or animal membrane.
3.	Setting	Particles do not settle down on keeping.	Particles do not settle down on their own but can be made to settle down by centrifugation.	Particles settle down on their own under gravity.
4.	Visibility	Particles are invisible to the naked eye as well as under a microscope.	Particles are invisible to the naked eye but their scattering effect can be observed with the help of a microscope.	Particles are visible to the naked eye.
5.	Separation	The solute and solvent cannot be separated by ordinary filteration or by ultra filteration.	The solute and solvent cannot be separated by ordinary filteration but can be separated by ultra-filteration.	The solute and solvent can be separated by ordinary filteration.
6.	Diffusion	Diffuse quickly.	Diffuse slowly.	Do not diffuse.

1.3 Coarse Dispersions

1.3.1 Suspensions

Suspensions are a class of dispersed system in which a finely divided solid is dispersed uniformly in a liquid dispersion medium. Suspensions can be classified as coarse or colloidal dispersion, depending on the size of particles.

Typically, the suspensions with particle size greater than 1 mm are classified as coarse suspension, while those below 1 mm are classified as colloidal suspension. When the particles constituting the internal phase of the suspension are therapeutically active, the suspension is known as pharmaceutical suspension.

Depending on their intended route of delivery, pharmaceutical suspensions can be broadly classified as parenteral suspension, topical suspensions, and oral suspensions.

The following can be the reasons for the formulation of a pharmaceutical suspension:

1. The drug is insoluble in the delivery vehicle.
2. To mask the bitter taste of the drug.
3. To increase drug stability.
4. To achieve controlled/sustained drug release.

Physical characteristics of a suspension depend on their intended route of delivery.

Oral suspensions generally have high viscosity and may contain high amounts of dispersed solid. A parenteral suspension on the other hand usually has low viscosity and contains less than 5% solids.

Ideally, the internal phase should be dispersed uniformly within the dispersion medium and should not sediment during storage. This, however, is practically not possible because of the thermodynamic instability of the suspension. Particles in the suspension possess a surface free energy that makes the system unstable leading to particle settling. The free energy of the system depends on the total surface area and the interfacial tension between the liquid medium and the solid particles. Thus, in order to minimize the free energy, the system tends to decrease the surface area, which is achieved by formation of agglomerates. This may lead to flocculation or aggregation, depending on the attractive and repulsive forces within the system. In a flocculated suspension, the particles are loosely connected with each other to form floccules. The particles are connected by physical adsorption of macromolecules or by long-range van der Waals forces of attraction. A flocculated suspension settles rapidly, but can be easily redispersed upon gentle agitation. This property is highly desirable in a pharmaceutical suspension to ensure uniform dosing. A deflocculated suspension on the other hand stays dispersed for a longer time, however, when the sedimentation occurs; it leads to formation of a close-packed arrangement resulting in caking.

1.3.2 Emulsions

An emulsion is a dispersion of at least two immiscible liquids, one of which is dispersed as droplets in the other liquid, and stabilized by an emulsifying agent.

Two basic types of emulsions are the

1. oil-in-water (O/W) and

2. water-in-oil (W/O) emulsion.

However, depending upon the need, more complex systems referred to as "double emulsions" or "multiple emulsions" can be made. These emulsions have an emulsion as the dispersed phase in a continuous phase and they can be either

1. water-in-oil-in-water ($W_1/O/W_2$) or

2. oil-in-water-in-oil ($O_1/W/O_2$) (Fig. 1.2).

The size of the dispersed droplet generally ranges from 1 to 100 mm, although some can be as small as 0.5 mm or as large as 500 mm.

Emulsions are subdivided arbitrarily such as macro, mini and microemulsions, based on the droplet size. In macroemulsions, the droplet size usually exceeds 10 mm. In the case of miniemulsions the droplets are in the size range of 0.1 - 10 mm, and in microemulsions the droplets are below 100 nm. Due to a small droplet size of the dispersed phase, the total interfacial area in the emulsion is very large. Since the creation of interfacial area incurs a positive free energy, the emulsions are thermodynamically unstable and the droplets have the tendency to coalesce. Therefore, the presence of an energy barrier for stabilizing the droplets is required. Surfactants reduce the interfacial tension between the immiscible phases; provide a barrier around the droplets as they form; and prevent coalescence of the droplets. Surfactants are mostly used to stabilize emulsions and they are called as emulsifiers or emulsifying agents. Based on the constituents and the intended application, emulsions may be administered by oral, topical and parenteral routes.

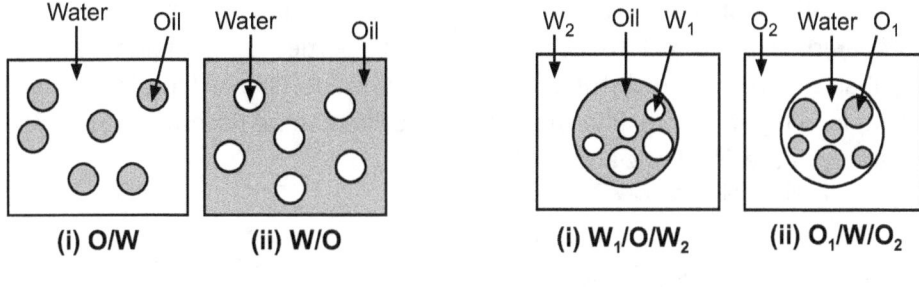

| (i) O/W | (ii) W/O | (i) $W_1/O/W_2$ | (ii) $O_1/W/O_2$ |

(a) Simple emulsions   **(b) Multiple emulsions**

Fig. 1.2: Different types of emulsion

1.4 Colloidal Dispersions

1.4.1 Micelles

Micelles are self-assembling colloidal systems with particle size normally ranging from 5 to 100 nm. They are classified as colloidal dispersion because of their particle size. Micelles are spontaneously formed when amphiphilic molecules are placed in water at a certain concentration and temperature.

Property of micellization is generally displayed by molecules that possess two distinct regions with opposite affinities toward a particular solvent. At a low concentration, the molecules exist separately in a solution.

However, when the concentration is increased, the molecules quickly self-assemble to form spherical micelles (Fig. 1.3). The hydrophobic portions of the molecules condense to form the core, whereas the hydrophilic portions constitute the shell or corona of the micelle. The concentration at which micellar association ensues is called the critical micelle concentration (CMC) and the temperature below which amphiphilic molecules exist separately is known as critical micellization temperature (CMT). The core of the micelle can solubilize lipophilic substances, whereas the hydrophilic outer portion serves as a stabilizing interface to protect the hydrophobic core from external aqueous environment. The process of micellization leads to free energy minimization of the system as the hydrophobic portions of the molecule are concealed and hydrogen bonds are established between hydrophilic portions in water.

Micelles are attractive candidates as drug carriers for delivering poorly water soluble drugs. Micelles can solubilize a drug at concentrations much greater than its intrinsic solubility, which results in an increased bioavailability and a reduced toxicity. Incorporation of a drug into a micelle alters, release kinetics and enhances the stability of the drug by reducing the access of water and biomolecules. Micelles generally have narrow size distribution and the size can be easily controlled by altering the formulation conditions. Due to their size range, they can be conveniently sterilized by filtration through a membrane with a 0.2 mm cutoff. Specific targeting can be achieved by chemically conjugating a targeting molecule on the surface of a micelle. Passive targeting to tumors can also be achieved due to enhanced permeability and retention effect (EPR effect). Tumors have leaky vasculature and inefficient lymphatic drainage system, which results in a greater accumulation of micelles in tumors compared with normal tissues. Desirable properties of a pharmaceutical micelle include small size, narrow size distribution, low CMC value (low millimolar to micromolar), and high drug loading efficiency. Pharmaceutical micelles can be used through various routes such as parenteral, nasal, oral otic and ocular.

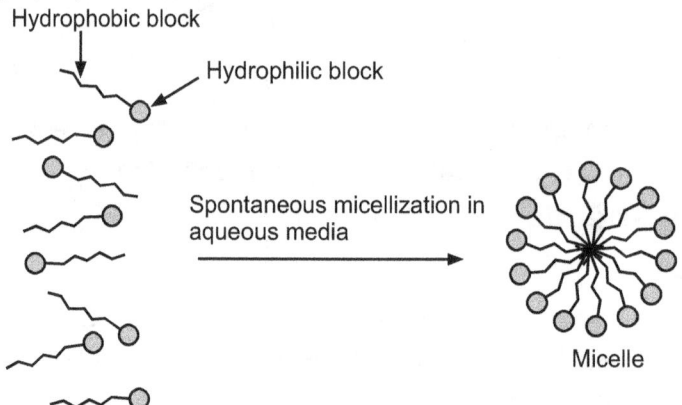

Fig. 1.3: Spontaneous micellization of amphiphilic molecules in aqueous media

1.4.2 Microemulsions

The term "microemulsion" was first introduced by Hoar and Schulman (1943) to describe a clear solution obtained when normal O/W coarse emulsions were titrated with medium-chain length alcohols. Since then, there has been much dispute about the relationship of these systems to solubilized systems (i.e. micellar solutions, surfactant-free solutions) and to emulsions. Danielson and Lindman (1981) define microemulsion as a system of water, oil and amphiphile which is (an) optically isotropic and thermodynamically stable liquid solution. The main difference between normal coarse emulsions and microemulsions lies in the droplet size of the dispersed phase. Microemulsions have droplets typically in the size range 10 - 100 nm and because of this small size range, they produce only a weak scattering of visible light and hence, they appear transparent.

Depending upon the phase volume ratio and the nature of the surfactant used, a microemulsion can be one of the three types:

1. O/W,
2. Bicontinous, and
3. W/O.

An O/W microemulsion is formed when the concentration of oil is low and a W/O microemulsion is formed when the concentration of water is low. In conditions where the volumes of oil and water are equal, a bicontinuous microemulsion is formed in which both oil and water exist as a continuous phase.

Microemulsions are thermodynamically stable systems. The driving force for their thermodynamic stability is the ultralow interfacial tension (10^{-2} – 10^{-4} mNm^{-1}). When the interfacial tension is this much low, the interaction energy between droplets has been shown to be negligible and a negative free energy formation is achieved making the dispersion thermodynamically stable. The large interfacial tension between oil in water, which is typically about 50 mNm^{-1}, is reduced by employing surfactants. However, it is generally not possible to achieve the required interfacial tension with the use of a single surfactant. Amphiphiles such as medium-chain length alcohols are added as cosurfactants to achieve the desired interfacial tension. Due to their amphiphilic nature, they partition between the aqueous and oil phase thereby altering the solubility properties of these phases. In addition, by interacting with surfactant monolayers at the interface, they affect their packing, which in turn can influence the curvature of the interface and interfacial free energy.

1.4.3 Nanosuspensions

Many of the marketed drugs and a large proportion (40%) of potentially bioactive molecules from drug discovery are poorly soluble in aqueous and non-aqueous solvents. Administration of poorly soluble drugs by oral route leads to decreased bioavailability because of the dissolution rate-limiting absorption in the GI tract. A traditional method used for solubility enhancement is the particle size reduction technique based on high shear or impaction such as milling or grinding. The use of this technique can be limited by high polydispersities in particle size, long processing times, and shear-induced particle degradation. Limited success has been achieved by novel techniques such as self-emulsifying systems, liposomes, pH-adjustment and salting-in processes. However, there is no universal approach applicable to all drugs. Nanosuspensions have emerged as a potential solubility-enhancing technique in the last few years as evidenced by a number of nanosuspension-based formulations in clinical trials and in the market. Nanosuspensions are colloidal dispersions containing drug particles dispersed in an aqueous vehicle in which the diameter of the suspended particle is <1 mm in size. The basic principle of this technique is to reduce the size of the drug particles to a submicron range. Reducing the particle size to a submicron range increases the surface area to be in contact with the dissolution medium and consequently the dissolution rate. Nanosuspensions have a number of potential benefits compared with conventional methods. Nanosuspensions allow to incorporate a high concentration of drug in a relatively low volume of fluid; provide a chemically and physically stable product; and can be used for controlled and targeted delivery of drugs. In addition, nanosuspensions can be used for drugs that are water insoluble (<0.1 mg/ml) and for drugs insoluble in both water and organic solvents.

1.4.4 Liposomes

Liposomes are spherical phospholipid vesicles that may range from 20 nm to a few microns in size. Liposomes can be made from natural phospholipids or their synthetic analogs. Liposomal formulations have been developed for a variety of applications such as diagnostic, vaccine adjuvants, and for delivery of small molecules, proteins, and nucleotides (Lasic 1998). The liposomes used for drug or gene delivery are normally unilamellar vesicles with size the range of 50 - 150 nm. As liposomes have an aqueous core, both hydrophilic and hydrophobic drugs can be delivered using liposomal formulation. The mode of incorporation of the drug inside the liposome depends on the polarity of the drug. Hydrophilic drugs are encapsulated in the aqueous core of the liposome, whereas hydrophobic drugs are entrapped in the phospholipid bilayer (Fig. 1.4).

Surface of liposomes may bear a positive, negative, or neutral charge, depending on the lipid composition and pH. Although neutral liposomes have lower clearance through reticuloendothelial system (RES), they have a high tendency to aggregate. Negatively charged liposomes are highly susceptible to endocytosis by macrophages. Positively charged liposomes, mostly used for gene delivery as polyplexes, interact with serum protein and are subsequently removed by the RES.

Liposomes, unlike micelle, are a thermodynamically unstable system and tend to fuse together and eventually separate out of the aqueous medium on storage. To achieve long-term stability, liposomes with high charge density have been prepared. However, high charge density of liposomes cannot provide long-term stabilization *in vivo* because of the presence of various proteins and enzymes. Another approach to stabilization of liposomes is coating the outer surface of the liposome with an inert hydrophilic. Such liposomes are called sterically stabilized liposomes. They have the ability to evade the immune system and hence can achieve longer circulation time *in vivo*. PEG is routinely used to provide steric stability to liposomes for drug and gene delivery.

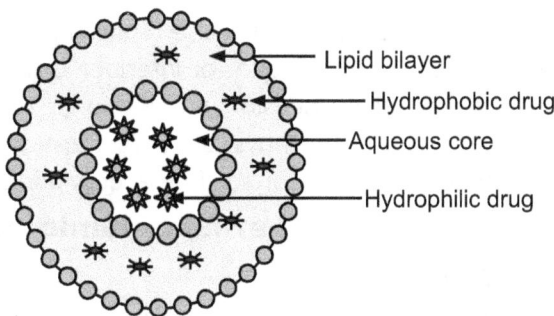

Fig. 1.4: Schematic illustration of localization of hydrophobic and hydrophilic drugs in a liposome

1.4.5 Nanoparticles

The advent of nanotechnology has opened new avenues for drug and gene delivery in last few years. A variety of nanoscale devices such as nanoparticles, nanotubes, nanogels and molecular conjugates has been investigated. Nanoparticles are the most commonly used nanometer scale delivery systems. They are typically spherical particles in the size range of 1 - 1,000 nm. The size of these delivery systems confers advantages such as greater and deeper tissue penetration, longer circulation time in blood, enhanced cellular uptake, ability to cross blood–brain barrier, and greater ability to target specific cell types. Drug or gene of interest can be incorporated in a nanoparticle by encapsulation or surface conjugation. Although majority of nanoparticles used in research have been developed from polymers, certain nonpolymeric materials have also been used.

1.4.6 Microspheres

Drug delivery using biodegradable polymeric microspheres has gained increased interest in the last two decades. Microspheres are solid, spherical devices containing the drug in a polymer matrix with size ranging from 1 to 1,000 mm. Microspheres are different from microcapsules. In microspheres, the drug is dispersed throughout the polymer matrix, whereas in microcapsules, the drug is the core surrounded by a polymeric membrane. Microspheres are widely used as drug carriers for controlled release and the incorporation of drug molecules into biodegradable polymeric microspheres has many advantages. The polymer matrix can protect drugs, such as proteins, from physiological degradation. Microspheres can control the delivery of drugs from days to months therefore reducing frequent administrations and improving patient compliance and comfort. Different release profiles with desired release rates can be achieved by selecting polymers with different degradation mechanisms. In addition, microspheres can be used to target drugs to a specific site. Microspheres have been proposed as delivery systems for traditional small molecular weight drugs, proteins, enzymes, vaccines, cells and even delicate molecules such as DNA.

1.5 Theoretical Considerations

1.5.1 Interfacial Properties

In pharmaceutical dispersion, the solid/liquid phase remains as finely divided particles in the dispersion medium. Therefore, a large amount of interface is involved in the formation, which, in turn, affects the stability of suspension preparations. The interfacial properties, therefore, play a vital role in modifying the physical characteristics of dispersion. The two most important interfacial properties include surface free energy and surface potential.

1.5.2 Surface Free Energy and Thermodynamic Aspects of Stability of Dispersion

A large surface area offered by finely divided disperse materials is typically associated with large amount of free energy on the surface. The relation between the surface free energy and the surface area can be expressed by equation (1.1):

$$\Delta G = \gamma \, \Delta A \qquad \qquad \text{... (1.1)}$$

Where, ΔG is the change in surface free energy,

ΔA is the change in surface area, and

γ is the interfacial tension between the disperse particles and the dispersion medium.

The smaller the ΔG is, the more thermodynamically stable is the dispersion. Therefore, a system with very fine particles is thermodynamically unstable because of high total surface area.

Thus, the system tends to agglomerate in order to reduce the surface area and thereby the excess free energy. Surface free energy may also be reduced to avoid the agglomeration of particles, which can be accomplished by reducing interfacial energy. [Fig. 1.5]

When surfactant is added to the suspension formulation, it is adsorbed at the interface. This will result in a reduction of the interfacial tension, making the system more stable.

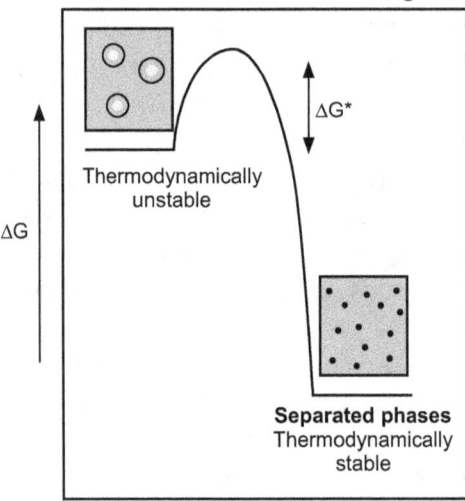

Fig. 1.5: Thermodynamic stability of dispersion change with surface free energy

1.5.3 Surface Potential (Charge on Disperse Phase)

The stability of lyophobic colloidal systems can generally be explained on the basis of the presence or absence of surface potential. This theory can also be extended to suspension systems. Surface potential exists when dispersed solid particles in a suspension possess charge in relation to their surrounding liquid medium. Solid particles may become charged through different ways. If the suspension contains electrolytes, selective adsorption of a particular ionic species by the solid particles is a possibility. This will lead to the formation of charged particles.

For example, in case of a dispersion of rubber particles in water, it may happen that hydroxyl ions (OH^-) will be more adsorbed than hydronium ions (H_3O^+) due to the asymmetric nature of the hydroxyl ion.

Occasionally, the surface active agents, which are already adsorbed at the solid-liquid interface, may ionize to give the particles positive or negative charge. Sodium dodecyl sulfate (SDS), for example, is anionic in aqueous medium. Solid particles can also be charged by ionization of functional group of the particles. In this case, the total charge is a function of the pH of the surrounding vehicle.

1.5.4 Electric Double Layer

When dispersed particles are in contact with an aqueous solution of an electrolyte, the particles may selectively adsorb one charge species. If the adsorbed species is an anion, the particles will be overall negatively charged. The ions that give the particle its charge, anions in this case, are called **potential-determining ions or co-ions**.

Remaining ionic species in the solution are the rest of the anions and the total number of cations added. This means, there will be excess cations than anions in the dispersion medium. These cations having a charge opposite to that of the potential-determining ions are known as **counter-ions or gegenions**.

They are attracted to the negatively charged surface by electric forces. Gegenions also repel the approach of any further anions to particle surface, once the initial adsorption is complete. These electric forces and thermal motion keeps an equal distribution of all the ions in solution. It results in an equilibrium condition where some of the excess cations approach the surface and the rest of the cations will be distributed in decreasing the amounts as one moves away from the charged surface.

Stern Layer: This situation is explained in Fig. 1.6. The part of the solvent immediately surrounding the particles will almost entirely comprise of the counter-ions. This part of the solvent, along with these counter-ions is tightly bound to the particle surface and is known as the Stern layer. When particles move through the dispersion medium, the Stern layer moves along with them and thus the shear plane is the one peripheral to the Stern layer. There are fewer counter-ions in the tightly bound layer than co-ions adsorbed onto the surface of the solid. Therefore, the potential at the shear plane is still negative.

Diffuse Layer: Surrounding the Stern layer is the diffuse layer that contains more counter-ions than co-ions. The ions in this layer are relatively mobile and, because of thermal energy, they are in a constant state of motion into and from the main body of the continuous phase.

Electric Neutrality: Electric neutrality occurs where the mobile diffuse layer ends. Beyond the diffuse layer, the concentrations of co- and counter-ions are equal, that is, conditions of electric neutrality prevail throughout the remaining part of the dispersion medium.

Thus, the electric distribution at the solid-liquid interface can he visualized as a double layer of charge. Stern layer, the first layer is tightly bound to the solid surface and contains mostly the counter-ions. The second layer is more mobile, containing more counter-ions than co-ions. These two layers are commonly known as the **electric double layer**. The thickness of the double layer depends upon the type and concentration of ions in solution. It is important to note that the suspension as a whole, is electrically neutral despite the presence of unequal distribution of charges in the double layer.

Two other situations may arise;

1. The concentration of counter-ions in the tightly bound layer be equal to that of the co-ions on the solid surface, then electric neutrality will occur at the shear plane and there will be only one layer of medium and ions, instead of double layer.

2. If the total charge of the counter-ions in the Stern layer exceeds the charge due to the co-ions, the net charge at the shear plane will be positive rather than negative. It means electric neutrality will be achieved where the electric double layer ends and the diffuse layer, will contain more co-ions than counter-ions. The charge density at any distance from the surface is determined by taking the difference in concentration between positive and negative ions at that point.

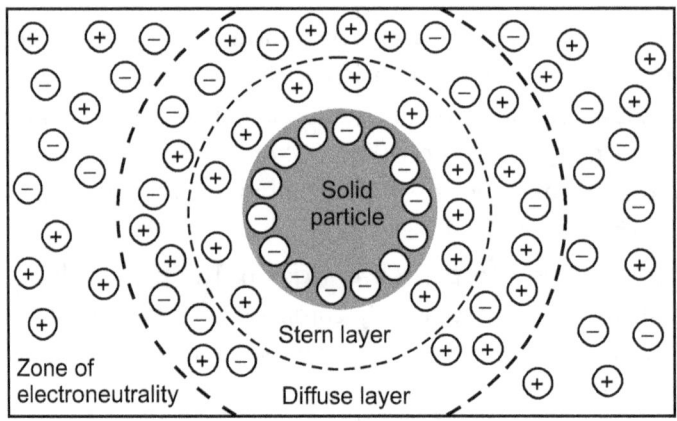

Fig. 1.6: Electric double layers at the solid-liquid medium interface in a dispersion system

1.5.5 Nernst and Zeta Potentials

The electric double layer is formed in order to neutralize the charged particles in a dispersion system. The potential in the diffuse layer gradually changes as one move away from a solid particle. This is shown in Fig. 1.7.

The difference in electric potential between the actual or true surface of the particle and the electroneutral region is referred to as the **surface or electrothermodynamic or Nernst potential (E)**. Hence, Nernst potential is controlled by the electrical potential at the surface of the particle due to the potential determining ions.

The potential difference between the shear plane and the electroneutral region is known as the **electrokinetic or zeta (ζ) potential** (Fig. 1.8).

While Nernst potential has little influence in the formulation of stable suspension, zeta potential has significant effect on it.

The magnitude of the zeta potential indicates the degree of electrostatic repulsion between adjacent, similarly charged particles in dispersion. For molecules and particles that are small enough, a high zeta potential will confer stability, i.e., the solution or dispersion will resist aggregation. When the potential is small, attractive forces may exceed this repulsion and the dispersion may break and flocculate. So, colloids with high zeta potential (negative or positive) are electrically stabilized while colloids with low zeta potentials tend to coagulate or flocculate as outlined in the table.

Table 1.3: Effect of zeta potential of stability

Zeta potential [mV]	Stability
from 0 to ± 5	Rapid coagulation or flocculation
from ± 10 to ± 30	Incipient instability
from ± 30 to ± 40	Moderate stability
from ± 40 to ± 60	Good stability
more than ± 61	Excellent stability

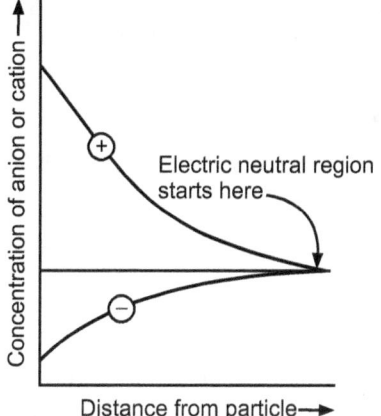

Fig. 1.7: Variation in concentration of cations and anions with distance from a negative charged dispersed particles

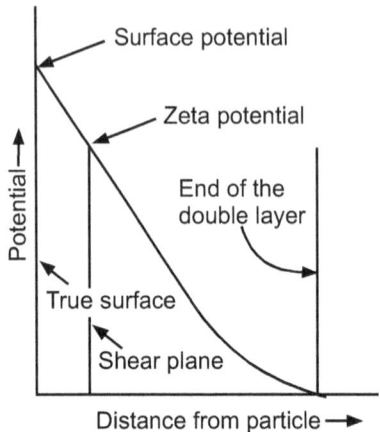

Fig. 1.8: The relation between nernst and zeta potentials

1.6 DLVO Theory

Particle collision in dispersion may occur due to Brownian motion or differential sedimentation rates. The consequence of collision would be either the formation of aggregates or redispersion of the particles. The outcome of collision depends on the attractive or repulsive forces between the particles and determines the quality of the preparation. As mentioned previously, zeta potential plays a very important role in stability. A minimum, known as the critical zeta potential, is required to prepare a stable dispersion system. A system with low critical zeta potential indicates that only a minute charge is required for stabilization and it will show marked stability against the added electrolytes. The precipitation of dispersion can be brought about by adding electrolytes. The precipitating power increases rapidly with the valence of the ions. This is known as the Schulze-Hardy rule.

Derjaguin and Landau and Verwey and Qverbeek worked independently and used the knowledge from Schulze-Hardy rule to describe the stability of lyophobic colloids (Derjaguin and Landau 1941, Verwey and Overbeck 1948). This is the classic DLVO theory, which explains the result of particle interaction in lyophobic colloids. The DLVO theory can also be applied to coarse dispersion systems.

According to this theory, the potential energy of interaction between particles (V_T), is the result of repulsion due to electrical double layer (V_R) and attraction due to van der Waals force (V_A) and can be shown by equation (1.2).

$$V_T = V_R + V_A \qquad \qquad \dots (1.2)$$

V_R depends on several factors including the zeta potential of the system, the particle radius, the inter particular distance, the dielectric constant of the medium.

Whereas the factors that affect V_A includes the particle radius and the inter particular distance.

DLVO theory can be easily understood from Fig. 1.9, Electrical repulsion due to the electric double layer and the attraction due to van der Waals force are shown in the opposite direction due to their opposite nature of force. At any distance from a particle (h), the net energy (V_T) is calculated by subtracting the smaller value from the larger one. When the net energy curve remains above the baseline, it represents repulsion. On the other hand, attraction can be shown by the curve below the baseline. The maximum repulsive value is known as the energy barrier. In order to agglomerate, two particles on a course of collision must have sufficient momentum to cross this barrier. As the particles overcome the repulsion, they agglomerate due to the attractive force and can be considered trapped due to van der Waals' London force.

Fig. 1.10 shows net energy interaction curves at different situations.

Curve A: Curve A exists when V_R is much larger than V_A ($V_R > V_A$).

In this situation, the dispersion will be highly stable because of the high net repulsive force. This dispersion is resistant to aggregation (i.e., flocculation or coagulation) as long as the particles do not sediment under gravity.

Curve B: Curve B explains a situation in which a high energy barrier (V_M), must be overcome by the particles to form aggregates. If V_M greatly exceeds the mean thermal energy of the particles, these particles will not enter P, the primary energy minimum. The minimum value of V_M that can create this situation corresponds to a zeta potential of more than 50 mV.

A very small interparticular distance is found at P. The high magnitude of energy at P causes the particles to bond tightly together. Consequently, it is possible that it will compact into a hard cake, which will be very hard to redispersion.

Occasionally, there occurs a secondary minimum of curve B at S, which is far from the surface of the particle. Loose aggregates can be created at this point, and this aggregate can usually be broken easily by shaking or dilution. The aggregation of solid particles in suspension systems can he termed either as "flocculation" or "coagulation".

However, according to the most generally accepted definition, flocculation occurs at the secondary energy minimum, S; and coagulation occurs at the primary energy minimum, P, of the potential energy curve of two interacting particles (Fig. 1.10).

Curve C: Curve C represents a situation where attractive forces predominate over repulsion forces all the time ($V_A > V_R$); and rapid aggregation will occur.

In addition to electric stabilization, steric stabilization can also be applied to prepare a stable dispersion. Substances such as nonionic surfactants, when adsorbed at the particle surface, can stabilize dispersion, even when there is no significant zeta. Therefore, the term for steric stabilization, V_S should be added to the equation obtained in DLVO theory, which gives rise to equation (1.3).

$$V_r = V_R + V_A + V_S \qquad \qquad ... (1.3)$$

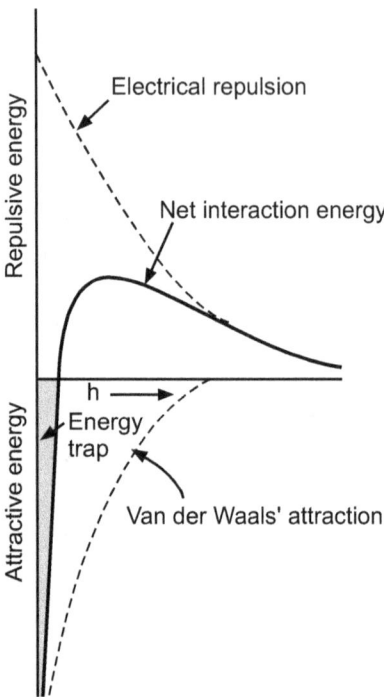

Fig. 1.9: Net energy of interaction between two particles as a function of inter-particulate distance

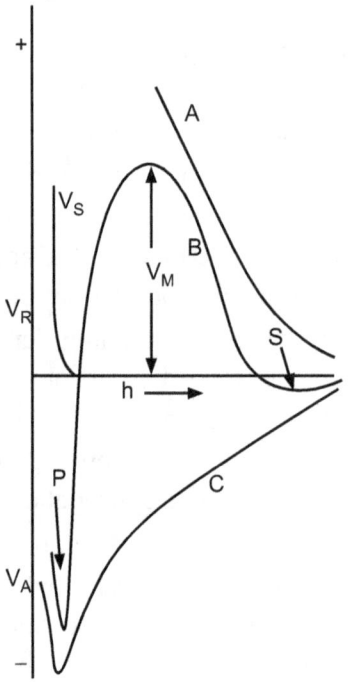

Fig. 1.10: Net energy nitration curve at different situations of attractive and repulsive forces

1.7 Kinetic Stability

Dispersions are unstable from the thermodynamic point of view; however, they can be kinetically stable over a large period of time, which determines their shelf life. This time span needs to be measured in order to ensure the best product quality to the final consumer. "Dispersion stability refers to the ability of dispersion to resist change in its properties over time."

These destabilizations can be classified into two major processes:

1. **Migration phenomena :** Whereby the difference in density between the continuous and dispersed phase, leads to gravitational phase separation:

    *   Creaming, when the dispersed phase is less dense than the continuous phase (e.g. milk, cosmetic cream, soft drinks etc.)

        Creaming, in the laboratory sense, is the migration of the dispersed phase of an emulsion, under the influence of buoyancy. The particles float upwards or sink, depending on how large they are and how much less dense or denser they may be than the continuous phase, and also how viscous or how thixotropic the continuous phase might be. So as long as the particles remain separated, the process is called creaming.

    *   Sedimentation, when the dispersed phase is denser than the continuous phase (e.g. ink, CMP slurries, paint etc.)

        Sedimentation is the tendency for particles in suspension to settle out of the fluid in which they are entrained and come to rest against a barrier. This is due to their motion through the fluid in response to the forces acting on them. These forces can be due to gravity, centrifugal acceleration, or electromagnetism. In geology, sedimentation is often used as the opposite of erosion, i.e., the terminal end of sediment transport. In that sense, it includes the termination of transport by saltation or true bedload transport. Settling is the falling of suspended particles through the liquid, whereas sedimentation is the termination of the settling process.

2. **Particle size increase phenomena:** Whereby the size of the dispersed phase (drops, particles, bubbles) increases

    *   reversibly (flocculation)

        Flocculation is a process wherein colloids come out of suspension in the form of floc or flake; either spontaneously or due to the addition of a clarifying agent. The action differs from precipitation in that, prior to flocculation, colloids are merely suspended in a liquid and not actually dissolved in a solution. In the flocculated system, there is no formation of a cake, since all the flocs are in the suspension.

    *   irreversibly (aggregation, coalescence, Ostwald ripening)

        Coalescence is a process in which two phase domains of the same composition come together and form a larger phase domain.

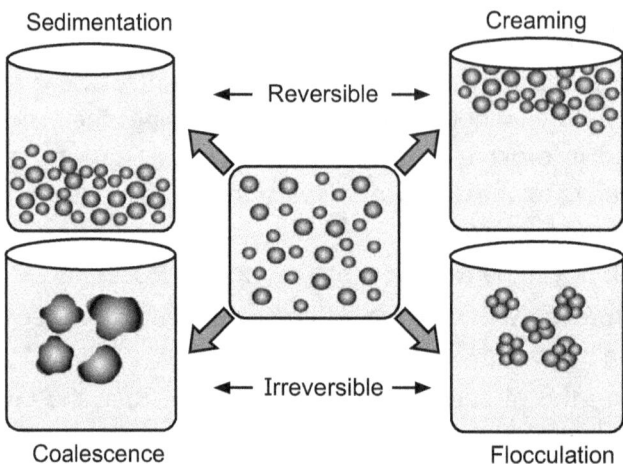

Fig. 1.11: Destabilizations of dispersion system

EXERCISE

1. Give classification of disperse system.
2. Explain in detail DLVO theory.
3. Write a note on thermodynamic stability of dispersions.
4. Write a note on kinetic stability of dispersions.
5. Write a note on electric double layer.

✍ ✍ ✍

Suspensions

Contents...

2.1 Introduction

The term "**Disperse System**" refers to a system in which one substance (The Dispersed Phase) is distributed, in discrete units, throughout a second substance (The Continuous Phase).

Suspensions are coarse dispersions in which insoluble solids are suspended in liquid medium. Suspensions are also called heterogeneous system or biphasic system which contains solid particles ranging from 0.5 to 5.0 micron. The solid acts as 'dispersed phase' and liquid (vehicle) acts as a 'dispersion medium'.

Pharmaceutically, suspensions are important formulation for oral, external and parenteral drug delivery.

Formulation of suspension presents many challenges to formulator because of their stability and packaging concerns. Even though Suspension dosage form is preferred and widely accepted for purely water soluble drugs for therapeutic application.

Principle :

About 70% drugs have poor solubility in aqueous solvent and such drugs can be administered only in the form of suspension, when enhancement of solubility complicates the process. Example: Aspirin, Paracetamol; which are class II drugs of Biopharmaceutical Classification System.

When solvents other than water are not acceptable to enhance the solubility, in that case suspension is the only choice and when the *"depot"* type effect is required then suspensions are preferred because insoluble solids act as a reservoir.

Quality Attributes of Suspensions:

Suspension should have following properties:

1. It should be physically and chemically stable.
2. Rate of sedimentation should be low.
3. It should get easily redisperse on gentle shaking.
4. It should settle slowly.
5. It should not form hard cake.
6. It should give uniform dosing while dose is removed.
7. It should have good organoleptic properties.
8. It should possess good pourability leading to ease of removal of dose from bottle.
9. It should not give microbial contamination.

2.1.1 Classification of Suspensions

1. **Based on General Classes:**

   Oral suspension: E.g. Paracetamol suspension

   Externally applied suspension: E.g. Calamine lotion

   Parenteral suspension: E.g. Procaine penicillin G

2. **Based on Proportion of Solid Particles:**

   Dilute suspension: (2 to10%w/v solid):

   E.g. Cortisone acetate, Predinisolone acetate

   Concentrated suspension: (50%w/v solid):

   E.g. Zinc Oxide Suspension

3. **Based on Electrokinetic Nature of Solid Particles:**

   Flocculated suspension

   Deflocculated suspension

4. **Based on Size of Solid Particles:**

   Colloidal suspensions (< 1 micron): Suspensions having particle sizes of suspended solid less than about 1 micron in size are called as colloidal suspensions.

   Coarse suspensions (>1 micron): Suspensions having particle sizes of greater than about 1 micron in diameter are called as coarse suspensions.

2.2 Floculated System and Defloculated System

Flocculated System:

In this system, particles aggregate themselves by physical bridging. These flocs are light, fluffy conglomerate, which are held together by weak van der Waal's forces of attraction.

If the aggregate is an open network, it is called **floccule**. They are fibrous, fluffy, open network of particles. It is loosely packed after sedimentation.

If the aggregate is closed one, it is called **coagule**. They are tightly packed, produced by surface film bonding.

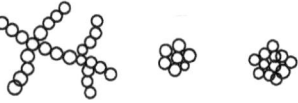

Floccule   Coagule

Fig. 2.1: Flocule and Coagule

In this, the sedimentation depends not only on the size of the flocs but also on the porosity of flocs.

In flocculated suspension the loose structure of the rapidly sedimenting flocs tends to preserve in the sediment, which contains an appreciable amount of entrapped liquid. The volume of final sediment is thus relatively large and is easily redispersed by agitation.

The Flocculated system is the system in which:

1. Particles exist as loose aggregates called floccules.
2. A some concentration of added ion, the electrical forces of repulsion are lowered and the forces of attraction predominates and under these conditions particles comes close together and forms loose aggregates. Particles experience attractive forces.
3. Electrolytes, surfactants and polymers are commonly used as flocculating agents.
4. Sediment of floc is rapidly formed, as flocs are the collection of smaller particles.
5. The sedimentation rate of floc is high. But sediment is a loosely packed network and hard cake cannot form.
6. Sediment is easy to redisperse.
7. Supernatant is clear.
8. Floccules stick to the sides of the bottle.
9. Flocculated suspensions are not pleasant in appearance.
10. In the potential energy curves, it represents the secondary minimum.
11. Bioavailability is comparatively less.

Deflocculated System:

In deflocculated suspension, individual particles are settling, so rate of sedimentation is slow which prevents entrapping of liquid medium which makes it difficult to re-disperse by agitation.

This phenomenon is also called as '**cracking**' or '**claying**'. In deflocculated suspension larger particles settle fast, and smaller remain in supernatant liquid. So supernatant appears cloudy whereby in flocculated suspension, even the smallest particles are involved in flocs, hence the supernatant does not appear cloudy.

The Deflocculated system is the system in which:

1. Particles exist as a separate entity, because of uniform dispersion of particles, particles experience repulsive forces.
2. Sediment of particles is slowly formed. As sizes of particles are small and particles settles separately and independently.
3. The sedimentation rate is low. But sediment is closely packed and hard cake is formed.
4. Sediment is not easy to redisperse.
5. Supernatant remains cloudy.
6. Particles do not stick to the sides of the bottle.
7. Suspension is pleasant in appearance.
8. In the potential energy curves, it represents the primary minimum.
9. Bioavailability is relatively high.

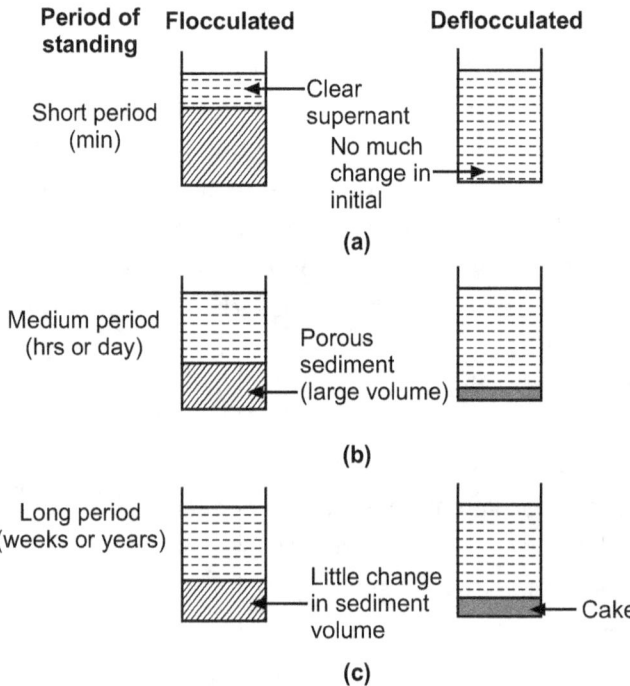

Fig 2.2 : Sedimentation behaviour of floculated and de-floculated suspension

2.3 Stokes Law

In most pharmaceutical suspensions, if the particles are large, they can not remain suspended. In general, particles are not in state of Brownian movement because of large particle size and high viscosity of the medium. Brownian movement can be seen if the particle size about 2 to 5 µm but at the same time particle density and medium viscosity should be favourable. The theory of Brownian movement proposes particle size and viscosity as the major factors. The rate of sedimentation of particles can be expressed by the Stoke's law, using the following formula:

$$\text{Sedimentation rate} \ = \ \frac{d^2 \, (\rho_s - \rho_l)g}{18 \, \eta}$$

Where d - is the particle diameter in **cm**,

ρ_s, ρ_l - are densities of a particle and liquid in **g/cm³** respectively,

g is the acceleration of gravity **(980.7 cm/sec²)**,

η is the viscosity of the medium in **poise**,

Stock's law is applicable if:

(i)   Particles are spherical; but particles in the suspension are largely irregular.

(ii) Particles settle freely and independently.

In suspensions containing 0.5 - 2 % (w/v) solid, the particles do not interfere with each other during sedimentation - hence free settling occurs.

Most pharmaceutical suspensions contain 5 - 10 % or higher percentages of solid. In such cases, particles interfere with one another as they fall – and hence experience hindered settling and not a free settling due to which Stoke's law is no longer applicable.

Stoke's law is applicable to deflocculated systems, because particles settle independently. However, the study of equation helps in successful formulation of suspensions.

As per stokes law following factors must be studied -

1.   **Particle size :** According to Stoke's law:

Rate of sedimentation $\propto$ (Diameter of particle)^2

So smaller the particle size more stable the suspension. The particles are made fine either by **dry milling** prior to suspension or **wet-milling** of the final suspension in a colloid mill or a homogenizer. Small particles facilitate rapid absorption.

2.   **Viscosity of the medium:** According to Stoke's law:

Rate of sedimentation $\propto \dfrac{1}{(\text{Viscosity of the medium})}$.

The viscosity of suspension should be optimum. Viscosity can be increased by adding suspending agents or thickening agents. Selection of high viscosity has both advantages and disadvantages.

Advantages of High Viscosity:

   (i)   Higher viscosity retards sedimentation rate, hence enhances the physical stability of the suspension.

   (ii) Inhibits crystal growth, because movement of particles is diminished.

   (iii) Prevents the transformation of metastable crystals to stable crystals.

Disadvantages of High Viscosity:

   (i)   Redispersibility of the suspension will be difficult on shaking due to high viscosity.

   (ii) Pouring out of the suspension from the container may be difficult.

   (iii) Creates problems in the handling of materials during manufacture.

   (iv) May retard absorption of drugs from the suspension.

   (v)   High viscosity may decrease patient compliance.

   3.   Density: According to Stoke's law:

   Rate of sedimentation $\propto$ (Density of solid – Density of liquid medium)

Lesser the difference between the densities of solid particles and liquid medium, slower is the rate of sedimentation. In pharmacy, solids having density 1.5 to 2.0 g/cc are generally used.

If the density of the particles is greater than the continuous medium, the particles will settle downwards, the phenomenon is known as Sedimentation. If the density of particle is lesser than that of the liquid medium then the particles will move upward, the phenomenon is known as Creaming. According to equation, rate of settling will be zero if density of solids and density of liquid medium is equal.

Density can be manipulated by addition of nonionic substances such as sorbitol, polyvinylpyrrolidone (PVP), glycerin, sugar, or polyethyleneglycols or combination of these.

2.4 Formulation Development

There are various problems associated with the suspension as far as the formulation is concerned. As formulation is the base of stability, because properly formulated suspension can only bring the stability to the suspension. Any problem in formulation leads to the caking, sedimentation, crystal growth.

So the formulator must take the kind consideration of the following parameters while developing the dosage form i.e. Suspension.

Particle Size :

Particle size plays an important role in the manufacturing of suspension. An ideal suspension is one with small uniform size particles which remains suspended uniformly without settling. Small size particles ensures slow rate of sedimentation, easy application, helps in penetration through the skin and hence gives faster rate of dissolution.

The concept of particle size is essential in every respect such as -

   •   For oral suspensions ease of administration depends upon particle size and shape.

- For parenteral use suspensions should have a small particle size so that it can pass through the needle.
- For ophthalmic suspensions large particles will induce pain, irritation and discomfort.
- For topical use, particle size should be small to avoid greety feeling to the skin and to cover a greater area of application.

The particle size of suspended drug should not go beyond 10 μm. It can be reduced by various types of size reduction equipments such as Hammer mill, Ball mill, Jet mill, Vibratory mill etc.

Viscosity :

Viscosity is an important parameter for stability and pourability. Due to sedimentation, suspension offers least stability amongst all dosage forms. So it is essential to decrease the sedimentation by increasing the viscosity. As viscosity increases sedimentation decreases, because viscous medium offers resistance to settling particles, particles settles slowly and they remain dispersed for a longer period of time.

The viscosity of the suspension should be optimum to yield stable and easily pourable suspensions, because as viscosity increases, its pourability decreases and patient may face inconvenience in removal of doses from the bottle.

Various types of suspending agents such as natural, semi-synthetic and synthetic are used to impart viscosity to the medium. Now a day's structured vehicles are used to solve the problem associated with viscosity, as they posseses thixotropic behaviour, i.e. gel-sol-gel.

Wetting :

Some drugs do not readily wet with water and the lumps of drug float on the surface of liquid. This occurs due to entrapment of air around the drug particle and leads to increase in solid–liquid interfacial tension. So to reduce the tension, surfactants are added to the formulation, sufactants having HLB value 7-9 are useful in concentration upto 0.1 %.

Second approach of inducing wetting is levigation. Viscous co-solvents such as sorbitol, propylene glycol and glycerine are used. When solid–liquid interfacial tension decreases, contact angle between these two also decreases and wetting occurs. Wetting agents like Tweens and Spans for oral administration and sodium lauryl sulphate for external use are preferred.

In addition to above parameters the first step in the systematic development of any pharmaceutical dosage form is the careful examination of preformulation test result. "The compilation of physicochemical properties" is known as **preformulation**. The use of preformulation parameters maximizes the chances of success in formulating an acceptable, safe, efficacious and stable product.

The preformulation study include various parameters like purity of the drug, particle size, shape, surface area, static charge, hygroscopicity, partition coefficient, ionisation constant, crystal properties, solubility, polymorphism, dissolution, flowability, physical and chemical stability and excipient-compatability. But out of these, crystal properties, particle size, surface area, dissolution, flow characteristics and drug excipient compatability, are of prime importance in the formulation of the suspension.

With this, organoleptic properties are essentially studied to improve the aesthetic appeal of the product and to make it more compatible. The organoleptic qualities include colour, odour and taste and these can be improved by adding suitable dyes and flavours to the formulation. Colours and flavours should be compatible with each other. For example, pink to red colour for Rose water.

Crystal Properties:

When organic drug substances exist in more than one crystalline form, it is called Polymorphism.

Polymorphs may exhibit different physical properties. For example, X-ray diffraction pattern, solubility, dissolution, vapour pressure, melting point, crystal form, density, compaction behaviour, flow properties and stability.

Out of many forms, only one form is thermodynamically stable and others are unstable. Addition of unstable form may result in crystal growth, caking, reduced bioavailability and finally reduced chemical stability. Hence, in the formulation only stable form should be used.

Many solids can be prepared in the desired polymorphic form by selecting an appropriate solvent for recrystallization and the appropriate rate of cooling.

According to study, Cortisone acetate exists in four polymorphic forms but only one is stable. Temperature also plays vital role that, increase in temperature lead to increase in solubility, but when temperature decreases the dissolved drug tends to precipitate out and larger crystals are formed.

Various techniques like microscopy, infrared spectrophotometry, X-ray powder diffraction and thermal analysis are mainly used to study the crystal properties.

Particle Size and Surface Area:

Particle size and surface area influence several physical, chemical and biological properties of drug. The parameters like rate of sedimentation, content uniformity, taste, texture and chemical stability are dependent on the particle size. The relation between particle size and surface area is reverse one, i.e. as particle size reduces then surface area increases and vice-versa. Although decrease in particle size favours suspendibility, the high surface energy of micronized powder caused by the large surface may result in poor wettability and agglomeration in suspension.

The most efficient method of producing particles of optimum size is by dry mill but wet milling can be done in case of potentially explosive ingredients such as benzoyl peroxide. Other methods are micropulverisers used for oral and topical suspension, fluid energy grinding and spray drying.

Fluid energy grinding is effective in producing particle size less than 10 µm. Particles of desired size and dimension can also be produced by spray drying.

Controlled precipitation with aid of ultra sound produces particles of size less than 5 µm.

Several tools are used to monitor particle size; Microscopy method is capable of measuring particles of 0.3 μm or larger. The most widely used technique to measure the surface area is BET theory of adsorption using an inert gas as an adsorbate.

Dissolution:

The absorption of drug depends on dissolution rate and hence ultimately on the solubility of drug. So the formulator must have knowledge about the intrinsic dissolution of drug from which dissolution can be predicted. Intrinsic dissolution is 'drug's own dissolution rate in a given solvent'. It is expressed as 'mg dissolved per minute per square centimeter'. The dissolution rate can be improved by reducing particle size, or by addition of small quantity of surface active agent.

Flow Properties:

Good flow of powder is essential for mixing and for homogenous drug content. Powders with low density and static charges exhibit poor flow. Flow properties of powder are commonly expressed by the "static angle of repose". Angle of repose is determined by filling the container with powder then draining it from bottom leaving cone. A low angle of repose indicates good flow and vice-versa.

Drug Excipient Compatability:

Excipients must be compatible with drug. Various excipients like dispersing agent, wetting agent, suspending agent, flocculent, preservatives, antioxidant, colour are used for the final product development and should be tested for their compatibility before use.

Drug Excipient compatability is checked by (TLC) thin layer chromatography, differential, thermal analysis (DTA) and diffuse reflectance spectroscopy. In this study, the drug-excipients samples are taken and tested, when there is no or minimal degradation after 8 to 12 weeks at elevated temperature, then the excipients considered to be compatible and are choosen for final formula development. A change in physical attributes (pH, colour, crystal shape) of the drug suggest incompatability. In such cases, other sets of excipients should be taken.

After studying above parameters, the formulator has choice to prepare three types of suspensions i.e. De-flocculated suspension in structured vehicle, Flocculated suspension and Flocculated suspension in structured vehicle.

- **De-flocculated suspension:** It is a dispersion of drug particles in a medium containing wetting agents and which is been made stable by adding structured vehicles to decrease sedimentation.

- **Flocculated suspension:** It is a dispersion of drug particles in a medium containing wetting agents and which is been made stable by adding flocculating agents.

- **Flocculated suspension in structured vehicle:** It is a dispersion of drug particles in a medium containing wetting agents where the combination of first and second approach is taken.

Following are the special approaches which are used to formulate suspension:

Structured Vehicles:

Structured vehicles are used to formulate the stable suspension so that the particles remain deflocculated with the ease of dispersibility with a minimum agitation. Structured vehicles are prepared by the help of hydrocolloids. These vehicles prevents the formation of hard cake which is main drawback of deflocculated system.

Flocculation using Flocculating Agents:

Flocculating agents helps in formation of loose aggregates thus result in flocculation. They are,

- **Electrolytes** act as flocculating agents. They reduce the electric barrier between the particles, as evidenced by a decrease in the zeta-potential and formation of a bridge between adjacent particles so as to link them together in a loosely arranged structure.
- **Surfactants** both ionic and nonionic, have been used to bring about flocculation of suspended particles. Since these compounds may also act as wetting agents to achieve dispersion so the concentration necessary to achieve flocculation would appear to be critical.
- **Polymers** are long chain, high molecular weight compounds containing active groups spaced along their length. These agents act as flocculating agents because part of the chain is adsorbed on the particle surface, with the remaining parts projecting out into the dispersion medium. Bridging between these latter portions leads to the formation of flocs. Particles coated wih polymer are less prone to cake than are uncoated particles.

Flocculation in Structured Vehicle:

This is a combination of first two approaches, where flocculated suspension is prepared and suspending agents like carboxymethylcellulose (CMC), carbopol 934, veegum, tragacanth or bentonite have been employed, either alone or in combination to retard the sedimentation of the flocs. Although the controlled flocculation approach is capable of fulfilling the desired physical chemical requisites of a suspension.

2.5 Excipients Used In Manufacturing of Suspension

(I) Drug :

It is essential to ensure the particle size of drug to be suspended. Larger particle size gives gritty appearance to the formulation .The drug should have minimum solubility, maximum chemical stability and good wettability in the vehicle.

The drug should be mono-sized without change in particle size distribution or crystal characteristics throughout the shelf life of suspension.

Drug's with some solubility in vehicle could result in the crystal growth, when there is fluctuation in storage temperatures. Crystal growth can be prevented by addition of polymeric colloids and surfactants.

Formulation of suspension, containing diffusible solids is less complex than that of the indiffusible one. The particle size of suspended drug particle should not go beyond 10 micron (μ).

(II) Vehicle:

Suspension is formulated because drug is insoluble in water. Water is the choice of vehicle for oral liquids.

Syrup, sorbitol, glycerin are usually used with water either to impart body to preparation, or to improve palatability of the preparation.

The added co-solvents or pH of system should not change the solubility of drug in vehicle.

Suspensions administered by routes other than oral route may contain other non-aqueous or oily vehicles.

(III) Suspending Agents:

Suspending agents are also called as thickening agents.

The additives which increase the viscosity of the continuous phase are known as 'suspending agents'. Suspending agents act mainly by increasing the viscosity of external phase and hence added to decrease the rate of sedimentation of dispersed particles. In addition, some suspending agents also forms protective coat around the individual particles, making them less sensitive to electrolyte concentration. The ideal suspending agent should have a high viscosity during shelf storage and it should have a low viscosity during agitation so that the product shall be poured easily from the container.

Hydrocolloids like acacia, tragacanth, and cellulose increase the viscosity of water by binding water molecules and thereby limiting their mobility and fluidity. Many of them are protective colloids in low concentration (< 0.1%) and viscosity builders in relatively high concentration (> 0.1%). Suspending agents are selected on the basis of viscosity produced by them but in selecting suspending agents it is not only important to keep sedimentation rate in mind but pourability, spreadability etc. of the final product must be kept into consideration. For parenteral suspensions appropriate viscosity is required for their easy passage through hypodermic needle.

Suspending agents are categorised in a following way-

1. Natural suspending agents/Polysacchrides:

(i) Acacia :

Acacia is useful suspending agent which increases the viscosity of the dispersion medium and a protective colloid forms a protective coat around the dispersed particle.

It is obtained from barks of *Acacia senegal* and other species. It is also used as a food additive.

Acacia increases viscosity of water. Its 35% dispersion in water is used as a suspending agent. Acacia alone is very sticky, hence always used in combination with the tragacanth.

Acacia shows maximum viscosity between pH 3 to 9.

Acacia has high microbial count hence it is essential to add preservative.

Acacia contains peroxidise enzyme which leads to oxidation, so heating at 100°C destroys the enzyme and benzoic acid and parahydroxy benzoic acid is also added to preserve the acacia containing preparations.

(ii) Tragacanth :

Tragacanth is a better suspending agent than acacia.

It is obtained from *Astragalus gummifier* and other species of Atragalus.

It produces viscous but less sticky preparation.

Tragacanth in 6 % concentrated mucilage is used. It is effective in pH range of 4-6.

It is free from peroxidise enzyme but addition of preservative is required.

(iii) Starch :

Starch is used as ingredient of compound powder of tragacanth.

It is used with other ingradients because its mucilage is very viscous.

Starch is used in the form 2.5% mucilage in water.

(iv) Sodium alginate:

It is obtained from seaweed *laminaria*.

For the preparation of mucilage it should be wetted with alcohol or glycerine or propylene glycol to avoid formation of lumps then mixed with water using high speed mixer.

It forms viscous solution at pH 7 when dissolved in water.

(v) Compound Tragacanth Powder:

It is a mixture of Powdered Acacia (20%), Tragacanth (15 %), Starch (20%), Sucrose (25%) and it is used in 2% concentration.

2. Clays/Inorganic Agents:

(i) Bentonite:

It is very pale buff or creamy hygroscopic powder.

Bentonite is natural colloidal hydrated aluminium silicate.

Bentonite swells in water and its 2-5% dispersion is generally used as a suspending agent.

It has mineral origin.

(ii) Hectorite:

It is a magnesium silicate.

It also swells in water but absorbs more water than bentonite.

It is used for external preparation.

It has mineral origin.

(iii) Veegum:

It is colloidal magnesium aluminium silicate.

It is a creamy white powder.

It has a good hydrating capacity and is more viscous than bentonite.

3. **Semi-synthetic Suspending Agents:**

   (i) Methyl cellulose:

   Methyl cellulose is soluble in cold water, but insoluble in hot water.

   It is used for both internal and external preparation.

   Methyl cellulose is available in various viscosity grades depending on its molecular weight but only high viscosity grades MC 2500 and MC 4500 are used as a suspending agents.

   It should be used in the concentration range of 0.5 to 2 %.

   In this, hydroxy group in the monomer is replaced by methoxy group to give methyl cellulose.

   It is less susceptible to microbial growth.

   (ii) Sodium Carboxymethyl Cellulose:

   Sodium carboxymethyl cellulose is soluble in both cold and hot water.

   It is used for both internal and external preparation.

   Sodium carboxymethyl cellulose is available in various viscosity grades depending on its degree of polymerization.

   It should be used in the concentration range of 0.25 to 1 %.

   In this, hydrogen atom of methyl group is replaced by carboxy group.

   (iii) Microcrystalline Cellulose:

   It is prepared from acid hydrolysis of wood cellulose.

   These are the microcrystals of cellulose obtained from crystallization of high molecular weight polymer with molecular weight around 36000.

   It is dispersible in water and forms colloidal solution.

   (iv) Hydroxy ethyl cellulose:

   Hydroxy ethyl cellulose is soluble in both cold and hot water.

   It is obtained when hydroxy group in cellulose monomer is replaced by hydroxyl ethyl group.

   It is available in various viscosity grades.

4. **Synthetic Suspending Agents:**

   (i) Carbomers:

   It is high molecular weight carboxy vinyl polymer.

   It is used for both internal and external preparation.

It is used in the concentration range of 0.1 - 0.4 %.

It is also available in various viscosity grades.

It is effective in low concentration and resistant to microbial attack.

(ii) Colloidal Silicon Dioxide:

It is white, non-greety powder and used in the concentration range of 1.5 - 4 %.

Table 2.1: Suspending agents and their concentrations

Suspending agents	Concentrations used as suspending agent (%)
Tragacanth	1-5
Sodium alginate	1-5
Bentonite	0.5-5.0
Hydroxy propyl cellulose	1-2
Hydroxy propyl methyl cellulose	1-2
Carboxy methyl cellulose	1-2
Sodium carboxy methyl cellulose	0.1-5
Microcrystalline cellulose	0.6-1.5
Hydroxy ethyl cellulose	1-2
Methyl cellulose	1-2
Colloidal silicon dioxide	2-4

(IV) Wetting Agents:

Wetting agents aids in the reduction of interfacial tension between solid particles and liquid vehicle, thus producing a suspension of required quantity. Some insoluble drugs do not wet readily with water and forms the lumps. The poor wetting is attributed to the presence of entrapped air on the surface of solid which floats on the surface of the liquid, and develop an angle of contact. Wetting is achieved by adding a suitable wetting agent which is adsorbed at the solid/liquid interface. Wetting agents orients in such way that the affinity of the particles for the surrounding medium is increased and inter particulate forces are decreased.

To ensure, satisfactory wetting and escape of entrapped air, from liquid preparation solid -liquid interfacial energy must be reduced, and for this purpose surfactants having HLB 7-9 are useful in concentration upto 0.1 %. Surfactants added as wetting agents can bring the flocculation.

For oral administration, non-ionic surfactants - Tweens and Spans, are preferred.

The second approach to achieve wetting is levigation. Glycerin, propylene glycol, sorbitol are valuable levigating agents. These viscous 'solvents' flow into the voids/pores of the particles to displace air. Hydrocolloids, such as acacia, tragacanth and sodium alginate forms hydrophilic coat on surface of hydrophobic particles.

Following wetting agents are used in the preparation of suspension-

1. **Surface active agents:** Tweens and Spans, Sodium Lauryl Sulphate etc.
2. **Hydrophilic colloids:** Tragacanth, Acacia, Alginates, Bentonite and cellulose derivatives etc.
3. **Co-solvents:** Alcohol, Propylene glycol etc.

(V) Dispersants/De-floculating Agents:

Dispersants are polyelectrolytes. These are polymerized organic salts of sulphonic acid of both alkyl-aryl and aryl-alkyl types that can alter the surface charges of particles through physical adsorption. These are marketed under the brand names: Daxad, Darvan, Marasperse and Orzan.

Dispersants appear to function by producing a negatively charged particles or increasing the negative charge already present, in order to aid dispersibility. The reduction of cohesive forces between the primary particles through the repulsion of like charge helps to break-up flocs and agglomerates and also aids dispersion.

Dispersants do not lower surface and interfacial tension and do not create foam or wet paticles. Most of them are not considered safe for internal consumption, but only Lecithin is used for this purpose.

Dispersants increases the zeta potential, thus discouraging particles to break the energy barriers and come together.

(VI) Floculating Agents:

Floculation is aggregation of particles which is possible by the addition of   electrolytes, polymers or surfactants and they are called flocculating agents.

Electrolytes are employed when a large sedimentation volume of a product is envisaged.

The electrolytes should have a charge opposite to that present on the disperse phase particles so that when added to a suspension, electrolytes neutralises the charge on particles and hence reduction in electrical barriers between them.

The valence of the ions is responsible for the effectiveness of an electrolyte in flocculating particles.

Trivalent ions are one thousand times more effective, and divalent ions are ten times more effective than the monovalent ions.

TRIVALENT > DIVALENT > MONOVALENT

Commonly used ions are NH_4, K, Na, IO_3, H_2PO_4, BrO_3, Cl, ClO_3, NO_3, ClO_4

Polymers also act as flocculating agents as a part of polymer chain get adsorbed on the particle surface with the remaining portion projecting out into the dispersion medium. The commonly used polymer is the various hydrocolloids. They assist in flocculation and also helps in increasing the viscosity of the medium.

The protruding segments of polymer form bridges between particles producing a flocculated product.

Flocculated capacity of polyelectrolyte colloids depends upon pH and ionic strength of the medium.

Surfactants may also bring about flocculation of particles. Ionic and non-ionic surfactants may be used. Amongst two, non-ionic surfactants can be used effectively which act by adsorbing and forming bridges.

(VII) Structured Vehicles:

Structured vehicles are also called thickening or suspending agents. They are aqueous solutions of natural and synthetic gums. These are used to increase the viscosity of the suspension.

Methyl cellulose, carboxymethyl cellulose, sodium carboxymethyl cellulose, acacia, gelatin and tragacanth are the most commonly used structured vehicles in the pharmaceutical suspensions. These are non-toxic, pharmacologically inert, and compatible with a wide range of ingredients.

These structured vehicles entrap the particle and reduce the sedimentation of particles. Although, these structured vehicles reduce the sedimentation of particles, not necessarily completely eliminate the particle settling. Thus, the use of deflocculated particles in a structured vehicle may form solid hard cake upon long storage. The risk of caking may be eliminated by forming flocculated particles in a structured vehicle.

Note that, too high viscosity is not desirable and it causes difficulty in pouring and administration. Also, it may affect drug absorption since they adsorb on the surface of particle and suppress the dissolution rate.

Structured vehicles are pseudoplastic or plastic in their rheological behaviours.

Few examples of hydrocolloids are given below-

Non-ionic type: Methylcellulose, Hydroxy propyl methyl cellulose

Anionic type: Sodium CMC, Polyacrylic acid

Clays: Bentonite

Suspensions for oral use contains high amounts of Non-ionic type suspending agents because of presence of high amounts of solids.

Suspensions for parenteral use contains suspending agents in the concentration of about 0.5%w/v.

Structured vehicles are not normally considered for the preparation of parenteral suspensions, because of their high viscosity, such systems lack sufficient syringeability for ease of use.

Clays are effective in concentration range of 2-5 %, but preservatives are need to be added because clays promote microbial growth. Methyl paraben and Propyl parabens are generally used.

(VIII) Preservatives :

A suitable preservative is needed as the solvent is aqueous. Preservatives should be physically, chemically and microbiologically stable. It should be inert, non-toxic and compatible with other excipients of the formulation. It should be effective against wide range of microbial flora. Methyl paraben, propyl paraben, thymol, chlorobutanol, benzoic acid and sodium benzoate are commonly used preservatives in suspension.

(IX) Organoleptic Additives:

Even a well-designed topical pharmaceutical suspension with optimum efficacy, safety, and stability requires the aesthetic appeal necessary to ensure patient acceptability. To improve the patient compliance the following additives are added.

Colouring agents: Colouring agents improves the look/appearance of the formulation and also helps in patient compliance. Natural and synthetic colouring agents are added to the formulation. Added colours should be compatible with the flavours or vice–versa.

Flavouring agents: An unpleasantly scented product may result in poor patient compliance.

Flavours are added to impart palatability to the formulation and it may mask unpleasant odour of the formulation, generally fruit and sweet flavours are selected.

Sweetening agents: Sweetners are added to improve the palatability and to mask the bitter taste of the formulation. Sweetners should be colourless, odourless, chemically stable, non-carcinogenic, non-toxic and soluble in water and should not give bitter after taste.

Sweetening agents like sucrose, sorbitol, glycerol, sodium saccharine are used but they may affect the properties of formulation.

2.6 Preparation of Suspensions

There are two methods for the preparation of suspension i.e. precipitation method and dispersion method.

A suspension can be prepared by the precipitation method or by the dispersion method.

The precipitation method is tedious, complex and time consuming. This method is not generally used for the preparation of suspensions. The precipitation of a drug can be achieved by controlling the pH or by the use of appropriate solvents.

The most acceptable method for the preparation of suspension is dispersion method which involves the dispersion of fine particles in an appropriate vehicle.

Method of preparations can be subdivided into following two broad categories:

(I) Precipitation Method:

This method is divided into three types:

1. Organic Solvent Precipitation,
2. Precipitation Effected By Changing The pH of the Medium, and
3. Double Decomposition.

1. Organic Solvent Precipitation :

The fine particle size essential for parenteral or inhalation therapy is obtained by this method. Insoluble drugs can be precipitated by dissolving them in water-miscible organic solvents such as alcohol, acetone, propylene glycol and polyethylene glycol and then adding this organic phase slowly to distilled water under standard conditions, that produces a suspension having a particle size in the range of 1 to 5 μm. Harmful organic solvents may pose difficulty in removing.

Example: Prednisolone is precipitated from a methanolic solution to produce a suspension in water.

2. Precipitation Effected by Changing the pH of the Medium :

This method of precipitation is used if the drug is weakly acidic or weakly basic. Drug precipitation is affected by changing the pH. In this, a drug is added in a system of favourable pH and drug may be readily soluble at this pH. Once the drug becomes soluble, then the solution is poured in another buffer system to change the pH of the medium and the drug will precipitate out to form a suspension in the medium of the second pH.

Example: Estradiol is readily soluble at alkaline pH in alkali like potassium or sodium hydroxide. If a concentrated solution of estradiol is thus prepared and added to a weakly acidic solution of hydrochloric, citric or acetic acids, under proper conditions of agitation, the change in pH will precipitate estradiol in a fine state of subdivision.

3. Double Decomposition Method :

This method involves formation of water insoluble product by the reaction between two water soluble reagents.

Example: White Lotion NF is prepared by slowly adding zinc sulfate solution in a solution of sulphurated potash to form a precipitate of zinc polysulphide.

(II) Dispersion Method:

In this method, the powder form of the drug is directly dispersed in the liquid medium. The liquid medium should have good power of wetting the powder.

Suspensions can be formulated by any of the following three methods as:

1. De-flocculated suspension in a structured vehicle (external liquid vehicle) as the final product.
2. Flocculated suspension as the final product.
3. Flocculated suspension in a structured vehicle as the final product.

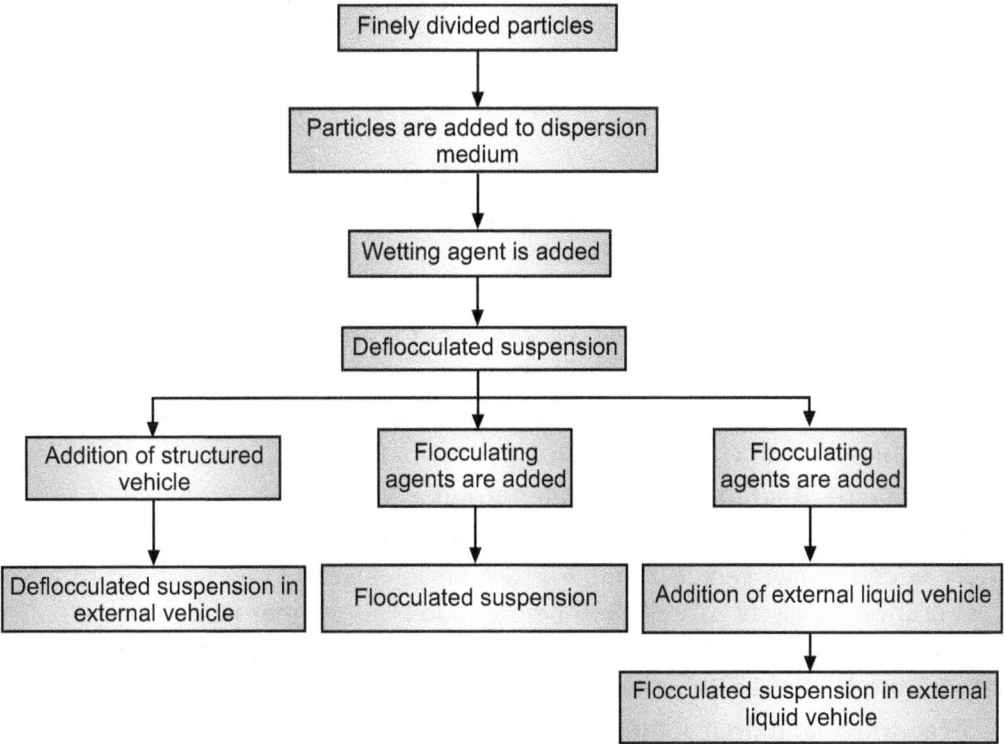

Fig 2.3: Flow chart of manufacturing of suspension

All three methods of preparation require uniform dispersion of the deflocculated particles and preparation of an appropriate vehicle.

The type of suspension to be prepared depends on the physicochemical properties of the drug and its application. Generally, a flocculated suspension in a structured vehicle as the final product is prepared for stability concern.

Following steps are involved in the preparation of suspension.

1. Preparation of a dispersion of the drug:

In this step, dispersion of drug in vehicle is prepared. Wetting agents facilitates uniform dispersion of drug in vehicle. So drug is dispersed in a vehicle with little quantity of wetting agent. Generally, anionic or non-ionic surfactants are used for wetting. Levigating agents like alcohol or glycerine may be used in initial stages to disperse the particles and to enhance the penetration of vehicle into powder mass. For small scale, Mortar-pestle and for large scale Ball, Pebble and Colloid mills, Dough mixers, Pony mixers and similar apparatus are also employed.

2. Preparation of a structured vehicle (external vehicle phase), followed by addition of the drug dispersion:

Structured vehicles are essential to decrease rate of sedimentation. Structured vehicles are aqueous solutions of hydrocolloids, polysaccharides or clays or combination of these. Warm or cold medium is decided on the basis of properties of type of agent used. High shear mixers or Eductors can be used to disperse the hydrocolloids in aqueous medium. Sometimes hydrocolloids are mixed with the water soluble ingredients such as citric acid and then this blend is mixed with other dry ingredients and whole blend is then slowly dispersed in water with high shear mixing.

- When this structured vehicle prepared in step-2 is added to above dispersion prepared in step-1, it will result in product i.e. *De-flocculated suspension in a structured vehicle as the final product.*

- When flocculating agent is added to above dispersion prepared in step-1, it will result in product i.e. *Flocculated suspension as the final product.*

- And when flocculating agent and structured vehicle both are added into the above dispersion prepared in step-1, and then it will result in product i.e. *Flocculated suspension in a structured vehicle as the final product.*

3. Addition of other excipients of the formula:

Other additives like antioxidant, chelating agent, humectants, preservative, fragrance and colour are added to the vehicle directly or are presolubilized in an appropriate cosolvent such as propylene glycol or alcohol before addition to the final volume. Usually, temperature-sensitive materials such as fragrances are added at low temperature and generally toward the end of the manufacturing process.

4. Deaeration, and final volume adjustment:

Final volume is adjusted with remaining volume of solvent and then to remove air and to make suspension pharmaceutically acceptable, the final batch is deareated by passing through deareating equipment hence excess air is removed.

5. Homogenization:

Now, suspension is homogenised by passing through homogenizer.

2.7 Formulation of Suspension

Some typical suspension formulae are given below.

(I) Suspensions Containing Low Solid Content:

Low Solid Content Suspensions are those which contain solids in 2-10 % concentration. These suspensions are also called dilute suspensions. These types of suspensions are required to prepare a model parenteral suspension as they have limitation for viscosity because of syringe ability and injectability constraints.

Example:

Sulphamerazine suspension	4%
Sulphamerazine	4%
Aluminium chloride	0.1%
Dioctylsodium sulphosuccinate	0.2%
Sodium carboxymethylcellulose	0.2%
Water, freshly boiled and cooled to make	100%

Sulphamerazine suspension 4% is an example of low solid containing suspension, so it would be best to formulate in flocculated form, electrolyte aluminium chloride 0.1% is added for the purpose.

Wetting agent i.e. surfactant dioctylsodium sulphosuccinate is needed in 0.2% concentration as sulphamerazine is known to be not fully wetted by water.

A hydrocolloid like 0.2% of carboxy methyl cellulose is added to slow the rate of settling.

Similarly, the organoleptic properties can be enhanced by adding suitable colours, flavours and sweetners to improve the patient compliance as it is a oral formulation.

By changing the additives, stability in formulation can be achieved if so required.

(II) Suspensions Containing High Solid Content:

High Solid Content Suspensions are those which contain solids as high as 50% w/v. These suspensions are also called concentrated suspensions.

Example:

Procaine penicillin G	20%
Procaine penicillin G	20%
Sodium citrate	1%
Sodium formaldehyde sulfoxylate	2.5%
Butyl paraben	0.15%
Lecithin	2%
Water, freshly boiled and cooled/ WFI to make	100%

Procaine penicillin G injection is an example of high solid containing suspension which is composed of 20% Procaine penicillin G. It is given intramuscularly hence it should contain minimum possible additives.

It is composed of antibiotic drug Procaine penicillin G 20%, it is buffered with 1% Sodium citrate to resist change in pH, and oxidation will be avoided by antioxidant like 2.5% Sodium formaldehyde sulfoxylate. Similarly preservative Butyl paraben 0.15% is added for the preservation of formulation from microbial growth. An ideal protective colloid Lecithin 2% is used to perform the dual action of wetting agent and flocculating agent.

The final product is first passed through a 40-mesh screen, then through a colloid mill, so that the Procaine penicillin G is uniformly coated with lecithin.

The product must be stored in silicone treated vials or cylinders.

Other high solid containing formulations are, Antacid Suspensions, Zinc Oxide Suspension etc.

(III) Antacid Suspension:

Antacids are intended to counteract the effects of gastric hyperacidity and peptic ulcer and to reduce the level of acidity in the stomach.

The reasons for acidity are spicy food, mental stress, unhealthy and irregular eating habits, smoking, drinking alcohol and carbonated beverages and bacterial infections.

Most antacid preparations contains water insoluble materials that act within gastrointestinal tract to counteract the acid or soothe the irritated or inflamed lining of gastrointestinal tract.

A few water soluble agents are employed, including sodium bicarbonate, but for the most parts, salts of aluminium, calcium and magnesium are employed that include aluminium hydroxide, aluminium phosphate, dihydroxy aluminium aminoacetate, calcium carbonate, calcium phosphate, magnesium carbonate/oxide/hydroxide.

All above mentioned antacid agents are not effective equally i.e. sodium bicarbonate, calcium carbonate and magnesium hydroxide effectively neutralizes the acid but magnesium trisilicate and aluminium hydroxide do so less effectively and slowly.

Various pharmaceutical agents such as carbonates, oxides, and hydroxides are used to neutralize the acid and maintain the gastric pH near to 4.

Liquid antacids generally are preferred than tablet forms because they do not require time for disintegration.

Each agent has potential for adverse effect:

Sodium bicarbonate is hazardous for patients having sodium restricted diet; it can produce sodium overload and systemic alkalosis.

Magnesium is hazardous for patients having diminished renal function and may lead to diarrhoea.

Calcium carbonate can induce hypercalcemia and stimulation of acid production.

Aluminium hydroxide in excess can induce constipation, phosphate depletion, muscle weakness and hypercalciurea.

Some drugs like tetracycline interact with the aluminium and calcium containing products, so pharmacist should counsel the patient regarding interaction.

Liquid antacid preparations should be pleasantly flavoured to gain patient acceptance. Liquid formulations are more preferred than tablets.

Type of Antacid Suspension:

There are currently over 200 marketed antacid suspensions. Although these products vary widely in composition, they can be divided into four types of suspension.

1. **Single strength suspensions:** These products have the capacities to neutralize 10 to 15 milliequivalents of hydrochloric acid per 5 ml dose.

2. **Double-strength suspensions:** Typically, these products have the capacity to neutralize 20 to 30 milliequivalents of hydrochloric acid per 5 ml dose.

3. **Antacids containing antiflatulent:** These products may be either single or double strength. However, they generally contain between 20 and 40 mg of simethicone per 5 ml dose.

4. **Floating antacid suspension:** These products usually have a low acid neutralization capacity. They also contain both soluble alginate and a carbonate-containing antacid which upon ingestion and contact with the gastric acid form a low density barrier that floats on the surface of the gastric contents. These products are specifically used for the treatment of reflux esophagitis.

Example 1: Magnesium Trisilicate Mixture B.P.C.

Magnesium trisilicate	5.0 g
Light magnesium carbonate	5.0 g
Sodium bicarbonate	5.0 g
Peppermint emulsion, concentrated	2.5 ml
Chloroform water, DS	50 ml
Water, freshly boiled and cooled to make	100 ml

Magnesium trisilicate is a weak antacid with acid consuming capacity of 15 mEq of HCl per gram and usually it is used in combination with other antacids. Magnesium carbonate is more effective and it has acid neutralizing capacity of 20.6 mEq of HCl per gram. Sodium bicarbonate also helps in acid neutralization. Peppermint emulsion is flavouring agent and act as a carminative as well. Chloroform is vehicle and preservative. This formulation does not require addition of suspending agents as magnesium trisilicate and magnesium carbonate are diffusible.

Example 2: Aluminium Hydroxide Gel

Aluminium hydroxide gel	36 ml
Sorbitol NF, or Mannitol, USP	7 ml
Methylparaben, NF	0.2 ml
Propylparaben, NF	0.02 ml
Saccharine, NF	0.05 ml
Peppermint oil, NF	0.005 ml
Alcohol, USP	1 ml
Purified water, USP q.s. to make	100 ml

Aluminium hydroxide gel tends to thicken or gel during their shelf life, this action of gelling accelerates when storage condition is 30-40°C. But this problem can be overcome by the addition of Hexitol (sorbitol or mannitol) in concentration from 0.5-7 % which depends on concentration of aluminium hydroxide in the preparation. This gelling in preparation can also be prevented by the addition of 0.1-0.5% sodium or potassium citrate. For the patients demanding for low sodium antacids, potassium citrate is preferred. The addition of potassium citrate decreases zeta potential which exhibits a maximum aggregation with resultant thinning effect.

(IV) Suspensions for Reconstitution:

Many official and commercial preparations consist of dry powder mixture for reconstitution or granules which requires the addition of water or some other vehicle at the time before use. These formulations are also called Dry syrups or reconstitutable oral suspension.

These formulations are prepared when the drug is not physically or chemically stable in aqueous form and when drug has limited shelf life.

Reconstitution powders have longer half life and they are stable physically and chemically as well. Not only this, but these powders are easy to handle than liquids.

Most drugs prepared as a dry mix for oral suspension are antibiotics, but in fact many other drugs can also be combined. For example :

1. Ampiciilin combined with Probencid for the treatment of rectal, urethral and endocervical infection caused by Neisseria gonorrhoeae in adults.

2. Combination of Erythromycin ethylsuccinate mixed with acetyl sulphisoxazole granules for the treatment of acute middle ear infection caused by susceptible strains of *Haemophilus influenzae.*

Formulation of Dry Powder for Reconstitution is formulated as below:

Drug: It is an antibiotic or combination with other drug. Mostly drugs are in insoluble state

Example: Ampicillin, Cefaclorr, Cefixime, Probencid etc.

Suspending agents: Methyl cellulose, Xantham gum etc.

Wetting agents: Tweens and Spans

Preservatives: Methyl/propyl paraben etc.

Stabilizing agents: Citric acid and sodium citrate etc.

Sweetners: Sucrose, Sodium saccharin etc.

Colourants: FD & C dyes

The dry mixture is either powder blend, granules or mixture of them.

Method of Reconstitution:

At the time of reconstitution, loosen the powder by tapping the container against hard surface.

Then add freshly boiled and cooled label-designated amount of purified water to the dry mixture in portions and shake until all of the powder has been suspended.

It is important to add exact quantity of vehicle to achieve proper drug concentration per unit dose.

Use within the prescribed period that in two weeks, after reconstitution.

Examples:

Ampicillin Oral Suspension USP, Cefaclor Oral Suspension USP, Doxycycline Oral Suspension USP, Erythromycin Ethylsuccinate Oral Suspension USP.

2.8 Evaluation of Suspensions

(I) Appearance and Organoleptic Properties:

Physical appearance of the suspension is evaluated visually in which consistency and sedimentation is observed. Colour, flavour and taste are observed by using sensory organs.

(II) Rheology:

For the stability of suspension, at different time intervals viscosity is studied by good quality viscometers, through which one can predict the timely behaviour of the suspension and its stability.

In suspension, for good flow and physical stability liquid must possess the thixotrophy i.e. gel-sol-gel behaviour. During storage, the suspension should exhibit gel like structure which become sol on moderate shaking for removal of doses and again gel on standing.

For such behaviour, suspension medium is largely responsible, where suspending agents such as microbentonite and CMC is used in combination than alone.

For the measurement of viscosity, various viscometers are used. Few of them are explained below:

1. Brookfield Viscometer: It consist of T bar-spindle which is lowered into suspension and the dial reading is noted which is according to the measure of resistance that the spindle meets at various levels in the suspension.

In this, T- bar goes down and indicates-

The pattern of particle settling with respect to time.

The level at which the flocs network is greater due to aggregation.

The prediction of ageing and storage condition.

A good suspension shows lesser rate of increase in dial readings.

2. Ostwald Viscometer: It is used to determine viscosity of Newtonian liquids. It is glass 'U' shaped tube consisting of two bulbs. Liquid is required to be filled in the upper bulb and time required for a liquid to flow by gravity from upper mark to lower mark of the upper bulb is measured. The viscosity is determined by using these time values and compared with liquid of known viscosity such as water.

Viscosity is determined by using following formula:

$$\eta_1 = \frac{\rho_1 t_1}{\rho_2 t_2} \cdot \eta_2$$

where, ρ_1 = Density of unknown liquid

ρ_2 = Density of known liquid

t_1 = Flow time of the unknown liquid (sec.)

t_2 = Flow time of the known liquid (sec.)

η_2 = Viscosity of known liquid

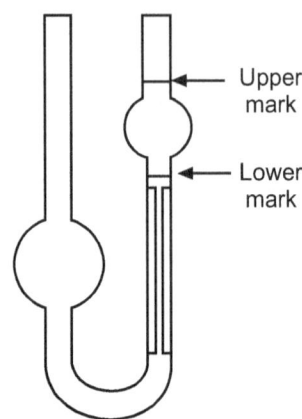

Fig. 2.4 : Ostwald viscometer

3. Falling Sphere Viscometer: It consist of cylindrical transparent tube with graduated section near the middle of its length, and steel ball is allowed to flow through the tube and the velocity of ball is measured and the viscosity is calculated using stokes law.

$$\eta \ = \ \frac{d^2 \, (\rho_s - \rho_l) \, g}{18 \, v}$$

where,

d = Diameter of the falling ball

ρ_s = Density of the sphere

ρ_l = Density of liquid

g = Gravitational acceleration

v = Terminal settling velocity

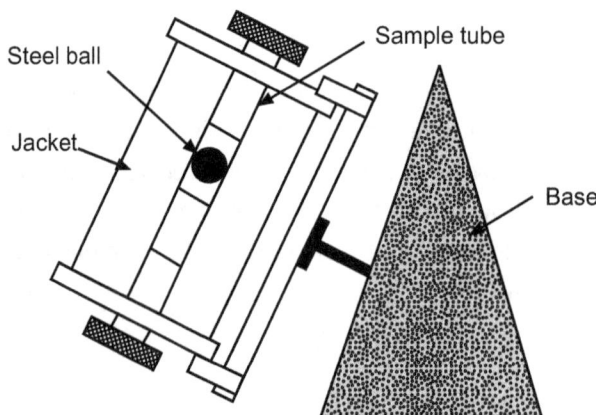

Fig. 2.5 : Falling sphere viscometer

(III) Particle Size:

Particle size of dispersed phase is an important parameter in stability of suspension. Change in particle size provides useful information related to stability. Measurements permit evaluation of aggregation or crystal growth.

Particle sizing can only be performed on diluted suspensions, although dilution may affect the aggregation behaviour of the sample.

Particle size and particle size distribution can be determined by various methods such as Coulter Counter, Optical microscopy and Sedimentation.

Particle size measurement can be rapid and simple or detailed and complex, depending upon the exact nature of the product.

(IV) Sedimentation Parameters:

The study of sedimentation includes two different parameters: sedimentation volume and degree of flocculation.

1. Sedimentation Volume:

In an acceptable suspension, the sediment formed should be easily redispersed to yield a homogeneous (uniform) product. The sedimentation volume F is defined as 'the ratio of ultimate volume of sediment (V_u) to the original volume of suspension (V_0).

For measuring sedimentation, volume measuring cylinder is used, suspension is poured into a graduated measuring cylinder and kept undisturbed for a definite time. Sedimentation volume depends on time and it is likely to differ with respect to time.

For example, initial volume of suspension is say 30 ml, and the final volume of the sediment is say 20 ml then it is calculated as

$$F = \frac{V_u}{V_0} \times 100$$

where

F = Sedimentation volume

V_u = volume of sediment and

V_0 = volume of suspension before settling

∴ $F = \dfrac{20}{30} \times 100$

∴ $F = 66.67\%$

This is how the percentage sedimentation can be calculated. Product is more acceptable when the value of F is higher.

Similarly, the Rate of Sedimentation can be estimated by the use of an Oden's balance. This consists of suspended pan in the suspension and it is counterbalanced against weight or attached to a pointer which moves on a rotating smoking drum. As particles settles on the pan it moves down giving an up curve on the drum or necessary weights are used to keep the original balance. This parameter gives an idea about time involved in sedimentation.

2. Degree of Flocculation:

Degree of Flocculation is 'an expression of the increased sediment volume resulting from flocculation'.

A more useful parameter to measure sedimentation is the degree of flocculation (β).

The degree of flocculation is calculated by using equation,

$$\beta = \frac{\text{Ultimate sediment volume of flocculated suspension (F)}}{\text{Ultimate sediment volume of deflocculated suspension (F}_\infty)}$$

Where,

(F) is sedimentation volume of flocculated suspension

(F$_\infty$) is sedimentation volume of the deflocculated suspension.

Sedimentation volume F gives only a qualitative account of flocculation, but β compares the sediment volume at two states, flocculated and de-flocculated. Therefore, the degree of flocculation is more important than the sedimentation volume.

(V) Particle Charge/Zeta Potential Measurement:

The surface electric charge or zeta potential is essential to decide the stability of dispersed phase system. Certain zeta potentials produce more stable suspensions because of controlled flocculation. Hence, zeta potential measurements give valuable clues to its stability.

It is measured by microelectrophoretic cell. In this, a sample of dispersed system is required to be mounted on a special microscopic slide across which a known potential is applied. The speed of movement of the particles across the field is a function of the zeta potential and is determined visually. The zetameter is a commercial micro-electrophoresis apparatus for easy, fast and reproducible operations.

This apparatus should be standardized using particles of known zeta potential.

(VI) Caking in Suspension:

Suspensions are thermodynamically unstable systems and when left undisturbed for a long period of time, it leads to an aggression of particles, sedimentation and eventually caking. Particles held together strongly are called 'aggregates' and the compaction of strongly adhering aggregates that settles at the bottom of the container forms a 'cake'.

Caking is the most difficult problem and cannot be eliminated by reducing particle size or increasing viscosity of the medium; once the cake is formed it cannot be remedied but can be anticipated and prevented.

When the particles are held together in the loose open structure, the system is said to be in the state of flocculation, these floccules settle rapidly but are readily redispersed.

To resolve the problem of caking, one must consider forces of attraction and repulsion between the particles in the suspensions. Flocculation and aggregation are brought about by the forces that reside at the surface of the particles. These forces depend on the nature of the species, distance of separation, orientation of the molecule, and the nature of the medium. Caking is well illustrated by DLVO theory.

To avoid the caking, it is essential to keep the particles dispersed and zeta potential is responsible for the same. A reduced zeta potential indicates instability. Certain zeta potential produces more stable suspension.

(VII) pH Measurement:

pH is an important physical parameter and fluctuation in pH is not desirable as some drugs shows maximum stability at a specific pH value. The measurement of the pH value provides good control over the manufacturing process and shelf life of the product.

The pH of semisolid formulations is determined by using digital pH meter.

The values should be taken in triplicate and then average values are calculated.

2.9 Effect of Particle Size, Polymorphic Form and Temperature on the Solubility

(I) Particle Size:

Particle size is one of the most important considerations in the formulation of suspension. The size of the solid particle influences the solubility because smaller particles offer larger surface area. As a particle becomes smaller, the surface area to volume ratio increases. The larger surface area allows a greater interaction with the solvent. So as particle size decreases solubility increases. The effect of particle size on solubility can be described by

$$\log \frac{S}{S_0} = \frac{2\gamma V}{2.303\ RT\ r}$$

Where,

S – The solubility of infinitely large particles

S_0 – The solubility of fine particles

V – Molar volume

γ – The surface tension of the solid

r – The radius of the fine particle

T – Absolute temperature in K

R - Universal gas constant

(II) Temperature:

Solubility is directly proportional to Temperature.

Temperature will affect solubility. If the solution process absorbs energy then the solubility increases with the increase in temperature. If the solution process releases energy then the solubility decreases with the decrease in temperature.

Generally, an increase in the temperature of the solution increases the solubility of a solid solute. A few solid solutes are less soluble in warm solutions. For all gases, solubility decreases as the temperature of the solution increases.

(III) Polymorphs:

When the substance crystallizes in more than one crystalline form it is called as polymorphism. It is possible that, all crystals can crystallize in different forms or polymorphs. If the change from one polymorph to another is reversible, the process is called enantiotropic. Polymorphs can vary in melting point.

Since the melting point of the solid is related to solubility, so polymorphs will have different solubilities.

2.10 Labelling of Suspension

Suspensions are biphasic formulations and may tends to settling hence containers should have adequate space to permit adequate shaking and to redisperse the sediment if occur. Container should permit the easy and prompt flow of dose from the containers during removal.

The suspensions must be labelled with secondary label "Shake Well Before Use".

In case of dry suspension powders, the specified amount of vehicle to be mixed may be indicated clearly on the label.

Suspensions should be stored in cool and dry place and should not be freezed, it may lead to aggregation.

EXERCISE

1. Define suspension and what is Stokes' law?
2. Differentiate between flocculated and deflocculated suspension.
3. Write short note on caking.
4. Write in detail about different formulation excipients needed for preparation of suspension.
5. Write short note on suspending agents.
6. Explain in details about different evaluation parameters for suspension.
7. How particle size polymorphic form and temperature affects the solubility?
8. Write a note on antacid suspension.
9. What are structured vehicles? How do they help in increasing the stability of a suspension?
10. Explain in detail about the low solid content and high solid content suspensions.

Emulsions

Contents...

3.1 Introduction

- **Emulsions** are defined as **'thermodynamically unstable biphasic systems consisting of at least two immiscible liquid phases, one of which is uniformly dispersed as minute globules throughout the other liquid phase, which is stabilized by the presence of an emulsifying agent.'**

- The liquid phase which is in the fine globules form is called the **dispersed phase or internal phase** and the liquid phase in which the globules are dispersed is called as **dispersion medium or external phase**. Globule size of dispersed phase vary from 0.01 µm to 100 µm.

- Emulsifying agent are the substances which reduce the interfacial tension between the two immiscible liquids. They adsorb on the surface of the dispersed phase of an emulsion.

- Emulsifying agents are also called as **emulgents** or **emulsifiers**.

Advantages of Emulsions:

1. Unpalatable oils can be administered in palatable form.
2. Unpalatable oil-soluble drugs can be administered in palatable form.
3. The aqueous phase is easily flavoured.
4. The oily sensation is easily removed.
5. The rate of absorption is increased.
6. It is possible to include two incompatible ingredients, one in each phase of the emulsion.

Disadvantages of Emulsions:

1. Preparation needs to be shaken well before use.
2. A measuring device is needed for administration.
3. A degree of technical accuracy is needed to measure a dose.
4. Storage conditions may affect stability.
5. Bulky, difficult to transport and prone to container breakages.
6. Liable to microbial contamination which can lead to cracking.

3.2 Applications of Emulsions

There are so many applications of pharmaceutical emulsions :

1. Emulsion permits the administration of liquid drug in the form of small globules rather than in bulk.
2. For oral use, emulsions help to mask the taste of unpalatable oils/oil soluble medicinal agents by dispersing it in the internal phase in fine globules and render the external phase sweetened and flavoured. For example, cod liver oil, castor oil, Vitamin A, D and K.
3. Emulsion provides rapid absorption of the drug since it is administered in the form of fine globules possessing high surface area.

4. Emulsions are better topical preparations than oleaginous preparations because of their less greasiness.

5. Medicaments which are irritating to the skin become less irritating if present in the internal phase of emulsified topical preparations than in the external phase.

6. A w/o emulsion can evenly be applied on unbroken skin since the skin is covered with a thin film of sebum which is miscible with the oil. It softens to the skin, since it resists drying out.

7. An o/w emulsion can easily be removed from the skin with water. Consequently, if water washable topical preparations are required, o/w type emulsions are suitable.

8. Intravenous emulsions are prepared to contain fats, oils, carbohydrates, vitamins and other nutrients to be administered as replacement therapy for patients who cannot take food by mouth.

9. w/o emulsion containing oil soluble drug provide an effective sustained release mechanism. These are injected by intramuscular route.

10. Emulsions are suitable to formulate foam aerosols in which propellant is emulsified with water or some other solvent system that contains the active ingredient.

11. Radiopaque emulsions are used as diagnostic agents in X-ray examinations.

3.3 Types of Emulsions

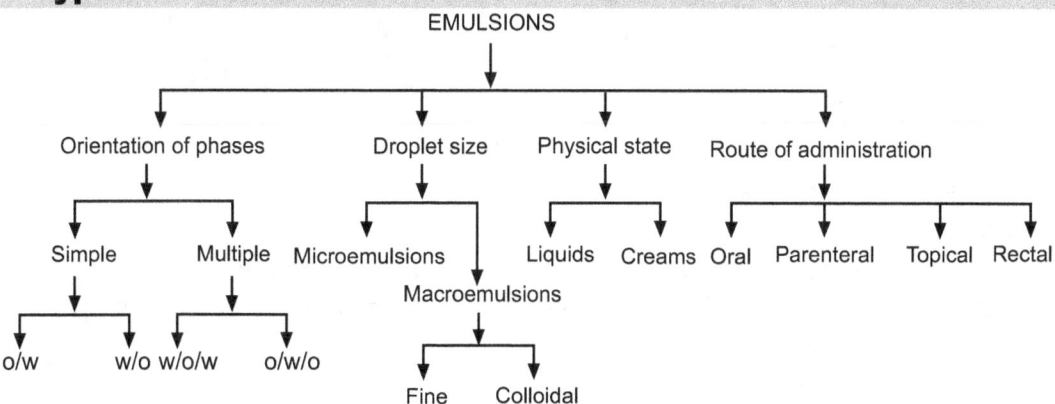

(I) Depending on the Type of Dispersed Phase:

1. Simple Emulsions:

(a) **Oil-in-Water (o/w):** In this type of emulsion, oily liquid is the dispersed phase and an aqueous liquid is the dispersion medium. These emulsions are preferred for oral/internal use because the bitter or unpleasant is masked by emulsification and oil being in a finely dispersed state is more quickly absorbed in the body.

(b) **Water-in-Oil (w/o):** In this type of emulsion, an aqueous liquid is the dispersed phase and the oily liquid is the dispersion medium. These emulsions are mainly used externally e.g. creams and lotions as the external phase is oil which forms an occlusive film and prevents evaporation of moisture from the surface of the skin.

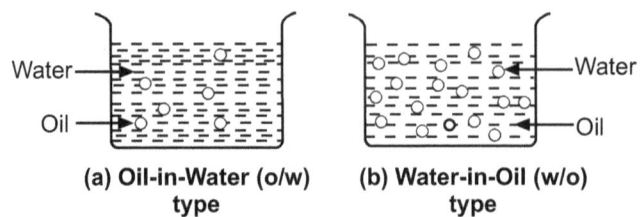

(a) Oil-in-Water (o/w)   (b) Water-in-Oil (w/o)
type   type

Fig 3.1: Simple emulsions

2. Multiple Emulsions:

These are of two types, o/w/o and w/o/w:

(a) Oil-in-Water-in-Oil (o/w/o) emulsion consists of very small droplets of oil dispersed in the water globules of water in oil emulsion.

(b) Water-in-Oil-in-Water (w/o/w) emulsion consist of very small droplets of water dispersed in the oily phase of oil in water emulsion.

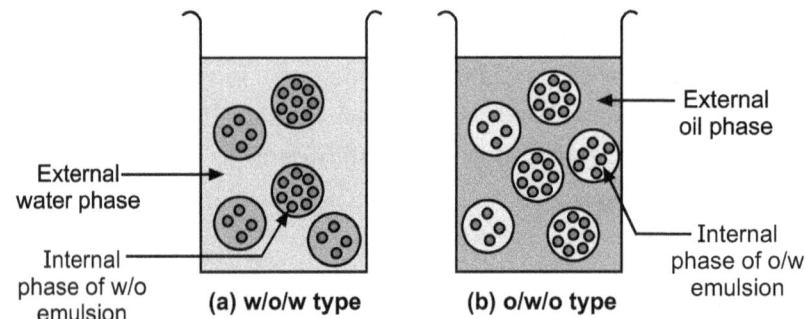

(a) w/o/w type   (b) o/w/o type

Fig 3.2: Multiple emulsions

(II) Depending on the Size of Globules:

(1) Microemulsions:

When the globule diameter is as small as 10 to 200nm, then the emulsions are called as microemulsions. They are also called as micellar emulsion and they appear as clear transparent solution.

(2) Macroemulsions:

On the basis of globules size macroemulsions are classified as fine and coarse emulsions.

When the globules mean diameter is in between 0.1 μ to 5 μ are called as fine emulsions and those with globules size up to 100 μ are called as coarse emulsions.

(III) Depending on the Physical State:

(1) Liquid Emulsions:

These are emulsions in liquid form. Liquid emulsions are used internally or externally. Most of the liquid emulsions designed for oral administration are of o/w type. Liniments, lotions and applications are liquid emulsions used externally and may be either o/w or w/o type.

(2) Semisolid Emulsion or Creams:

These are emulsions in semisolid form, semisolid emulsions are mainly used externally and may be of o/w or w/o type.

(IV) Depending on the Route of Administration:

(1) Oral Emulsions: These are mainly o/w type of emulsions.

(2) Parenteral Emulsions: These emulsions may be administered parenterally. Emulsion for parenteral use must have finely subdivided dispersed phase and the emulsifier must be non-toxic.

(3) Topical Emulsions: Topical emulsion may be either o/w or w/o type. e.g. liniments, lotions, applications and creams.

(4) Rectal Emulsions: Enemas are formulated as o/w emulsions.

3.4 Physicochemical Principles

- Emulsions are thermodyanamically unstable heterogeneous biphasic system consisting of at least one immiscible liquid dispersed in the other.

- Here, one phase is oil (non-aqueous) and other is water (aqueous). Both the phases are immiscible because cohesive attraction is stronger than adhesive attraction. These two different phases hence do not get miscible and tension at the surface begins to develop is called 'surface tension'. Due to unbalanced cohesive and adhesive forces there develop an interface and then interfacial tension.

- Emulsions can be successfully prepared by mixing two miscible phases with the aid of emulsifying agent.

- When liquid is broken down into globules it results in tremendous increase in the surface area and finally surface free energy. Such systems are thermodynamically unstable and may go back to its original state. So the formulator must have knowledge of forces operative in disperse phase system to formulate physically stable emulsion.

- A stable emulsion is one in which the dispersed globules retain their initial character and remain uniformly distributed throughout the continuous phase. Various types of deviations from this ideal behaviour can occur. To make the stable emulsion, certain physical and chemical parameters are essential to be studied.

- As far as the formulation is concerned, emulsion should have small droplet size. Addition of only emulsifying agent into the emulsion will not only stabilize the emulsion but small droplet size actually facilitates emulsification.

- Similarly, viscous continuous phase decreases the kinetic energy of the system and reduces the migration of dispersed phase globules and thus helps in prevention from creaming. Instability in formulation can be avoided by reducing density difference between the densities of two phases.

- It is ideal to maintain identical densities. The concentration of dispersed phase should not be less than 20 % which may result in creaming so it should be optimum. As much as 75 % dispersed phase can be included but more than 60 % of internal phase may show phase inversion.

- Emulsifying agent must protect the emulsion from breaking or cracking. Prevention from breaking is achieved by monolayer or multimolecular film of emulsifying agent. Moulds, yeast and bacteria can decompose the emulsifying agent.

- Generally, two or more emulsifying agents should be selected to increase the strength of the film. Strong interfacial film helps in prevention of coalescence. The system with higher inter droplet electrostatic repulsion does not allow dispersed globules to coalescence.

- Electrostatic forces can be adjusted by addition of electrolytes. The repulsion between two droplets makes the system stable.

- Incompatible ingredients could lead to cracking. For example :
  - Addition of alcohol precipitate agar, tragacanth (hydrophilic emulsifier) as these emulgents are insoluble in alcohol.
  - Addition of excess electrolyte changes electrostatic forces. Combination of cationic and anionic emulsifying agents produces cracked emulsion.
  - Excess dispersed phase results in collision of droplets and which may lead to coalescence.
  - Change in pH may also lead to the breaking of emulsion.

- Fats and oils such as wool fat, wool alcohol present in emulsion can be susceptible to oxidation by atmospheric oxygen or by the action of microorganisms. This results in degraded product. The problem can be remedied by addition of antioxidants.

- Adverse storage conditions i.e. increase in temperature will cause a creaming because of increase in motion of the droplets of dispersed phase and emulgents.

- Due to this effect, the disperse phase will enable the energy barrier to be easily surmounted and thus the number of collisions between globules will increase. Increased motion of the emulgent will result in a more expanded monolayer, and so coalescence is more likely to happen.

- Coagulation of certain macromolecular emulsifying agents may occur by an increase in temperature. Certain emulgents may also precipitate at low temperatures.

- At the other extreme, freezing of the aqueous phase will produce ice crystals that may exert unusual pressures on the dispersed globules and their adsorbed layer of emulgent. In addition, dissolved electrolyte may concentrate in the unfrozen water, thus affecting the charge density on the globules.

- The growth of microorganisms within the emulsion can cause deterioration and it is therefore essential that these products are protected as far as possible from the ingress of microorganisms during manufacture, storage and use, and that they contain adequate preservatives.

3.5 Theories of Emulsification

Many theories have been used to explain how emulsifying agents act in promoting emulsification and maintaining the stability of the resulting emulsion, amongst them few are most prevalent. These are as follows:

1. Surface tension theory
2. Oriented wedge theory
3. Plastic or Interfacial film theory
4. Charge repulsion theory
5. Steric repulsion theory

1. Surface Tension Theory:

- When one liquid is in contact with a second liquid in which it is insoluble and immiscible, the force causing each liquid to resist breaking up into smaller globules is called interfacial tension.

- There are some substances that can promote the lowering of the resistance to break-up and can allow the liquid to be reduced to smaller drops. These tension lowering substances are called surfactants (Surface-acting).

- According to the surface tension theory of emulsification, the use of surfactants results in lowering of the interfacial tension of the two immiscible liquids by getting adsorbed at the interface to form a monomolecular film, reducing the repulsive force between two immiscible liquids and reducing each liquid's attraction for its own molecules (i.e. cohesive forces).

- Thus, surfactants facilitate the breaking up of large globules into smaller ones which have lesser tendency to reunite or coalesce this leads to formation of a stable emulsion.

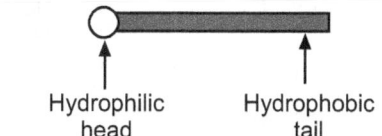

Hydrophilic   Hydrophobic
   head   tail

Representative structure of surfactant molecule

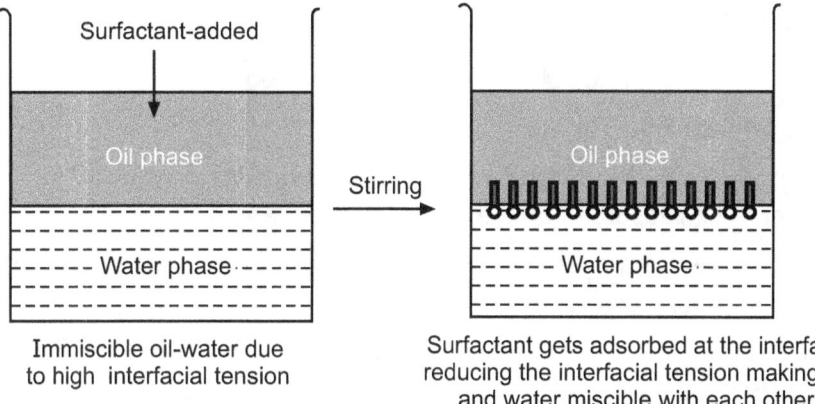

Immiscible oil-water due   Surfactant gets adsorbed at the interface
to high interfacial tension   reducing the interfacial tension making oil
                                  and water miscible with each other

Fig. 3.3: Surface tension theory

2. Oriented-wedge Theory:

- According to this theory, emulsifying agent (surfactant) get absorbed around a droplet of the internal phase of the emulsion. It is based on the fact that certain emulsifying agents orient themselves about and within a liquid depending on their solubility in that particular liquid.

- If a system contains two immiscible liquids and an emulsifying agent is added to that system, the emulsifying agent is embedded more deeply in one of the phases in which it is more soluble than the other phase. For example; soaps, which have a hydrophilic or water-loving portion and a hydrophobic or water-hating portion, orient into each phase according to their respective intimacy.

- Generally, an emulsifying agent having a greater hydrophilic character than hydrophobic character will promote an oil-in-water emulsion [Fig. 3.4 (a)]; and an agent having greater hydrophobic character than hydrophilic character will promote a water-in-oil emulsion [Fig. 3.4 (b)].

- This can also be explained in other way that the phase in which the emulsifying agent is more soluble will generally become the continuous or external phase of the emulsion.

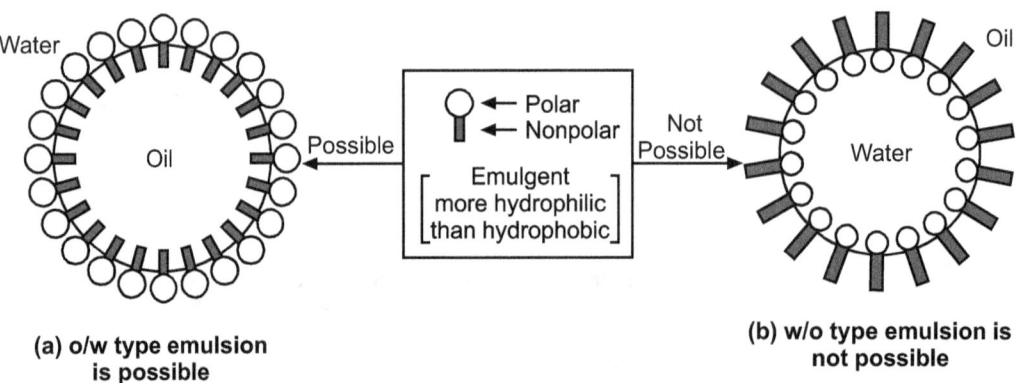

(a) o/w type emulsion
is possible

(b) w/o type emulsion is
not possible

Fig. 3.4 : Oriented wedge theory

3. Plastic or Interfacial Film Theory:

- This theory says that the emulsifying agent surrounds the droplets of internal phase as a thin layer of film adsorbed on the surface of the drops.

- The film of emulsifying agent will act as a barrier between the dispersed globules and prevents contact and coalescing of the droplets.

- Stability of emulsified system depends upon on the magnitude of strongness of the film formed over the surface of the globules. Tougher and more pliable the film, greater the stability of emulsion.

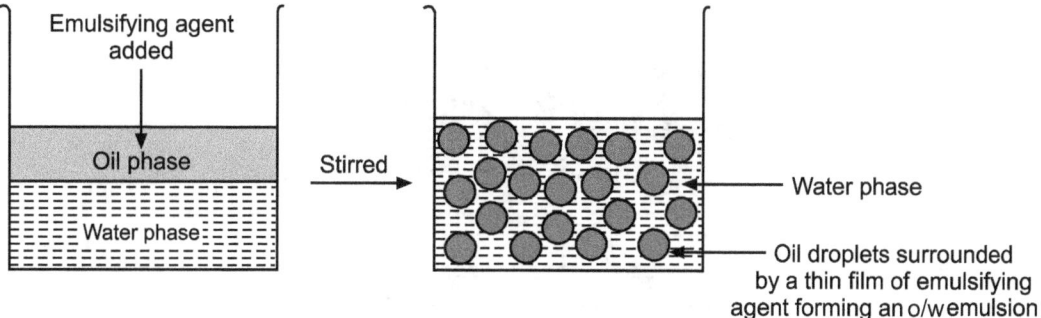

Fig. 3.5 : Interfacial film theory

4. Charge Repulsion Theory:

- This theory of emulsion says that, the fine globules of dispersed phase are separated due to the repulsive forces developed as a result of the nature of emulsifying agent (anionic or cationic) or by adsorbing ions from the dispersion medium, Fig. 3.6.

- The charge developed on the surface of oil globules is great enough to cause repulsion between droplets which acts as electrical barrier to prevent coalescence of the oil droplets and allow the oil phase to remain in droplet form, uniformly dispersed in continuous water phase .

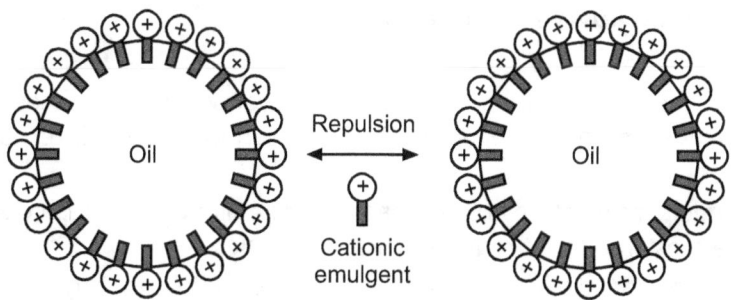

Fig. 3.6: Charge repulsion theory

5. Steric Repulsion Theory:

- This theory says that, the repulsion develops between the water droplets due to the long hydrocarbon chains of emulsifying agent which has been adsorbed on their surface. This repulsion is called *steric repulsion*, preventing the contact or coalescence of water droplets.

- This theory can explain the process of emulsification only in w/o type of emulsion.

- It is found that not a single theory of emulsification is able to explain the formation of different types of emulsion. It might be a collective theories to explain the process of emulsification.

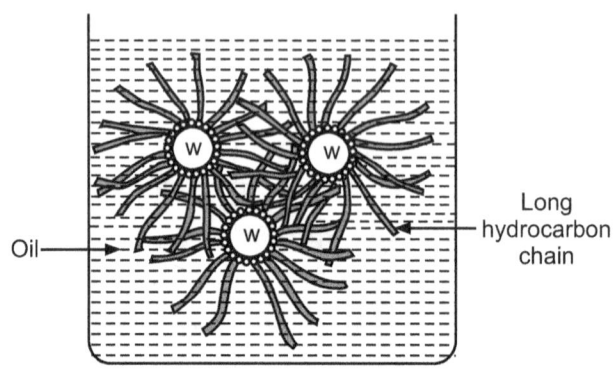

Fig. 3.7: Steric repulsion theory

3.6 Film Barriers to Coalescence

- The coalescence is prevented by effective use of emulsifier. Emulsifying agents concentrate at the interface and forms a tough film around the globule and acts as barrier to coalescence. Hence the choice of an emulgents is a critical factor since the quality and stability of the emulsion depends on it. Emulsifying agents can impart stability to such systems.

- According to mechanism of film formation, emulsifying agents are classified as:

  1. **Surfactants:** Tweens, Spans, Soaps.
  2. **Hydrophilic colloids:** Acacia, Gelatin.
  3. **Finely divided solids:** Veegum, Bentinite.

Film Formation

- To understand the emulsification and barrier to coalescence it is essential to study the orientation of the film of the emulsifier on the surface of the internal phase of an emulsion.

- The efficient emulgent must be able to readily form a film around each dispersed globule. It is one of the most important requirements of emulsion.

- Emulsifying agents acts as a barrier by their three film forming mechanisms, these films can be monolayer, multilayer or particulate one. But a good film should not thin out and rupture when sandwiched between the globules and if broken it should reform readily.

- Film produced, provides additional repulsive force and inhibits the close approach of droplets.

- Film also reduces attractive Vander walls forces.

- When this film is closely packed and elastic, it provides barriers to coalescence of droplets. Surfactant interfacial films also lower the interfacial tension of oil and water.

(I) Monomolecular Film

- Surfactant adsorbs at oil-water interface and form monomolecular film. The film rapidly envelopes the droplets as soon as they are formed. Monomolecular film should be compact and strong enough so that it cannot be easily distrubed or broken.

- These days combination of emulgents is used.
- Combination consists of hydrophilic emulgent in aqueous phase and hydrophobic emulgent in the oily phase. These two emulsifying agents interact to form a complex film. It is assumed that, in this complex film both emulsifying agents support each other and strengthen the monomolecular film. Surface active agents or amphiphiles reduce interfacial tension because of their adsorption at the oil water interface to form monomolecular film.
- In fact, the dispersed droplets are surrounded by a coherent monolayer that helps to prevent coalescence between two droplets as they approach one other.
- When two emulsifying agents are involved in film formation they must give close packing and complex film.

Example 1: When hydrophilic sodium cetyl sulfate and lipophilic cholesterol is used in combination, it forms close packed complex film at the interface which produces an excellent emulsion.

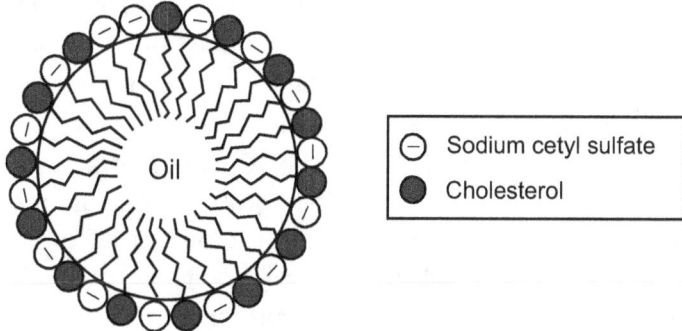

Fig. 3.8: Monomolecular Film of sodium cetyl sulfate and cholesterol showing excellent emulsion with close packing and complex film

Example 2: When sodium cetyl sulfate is used with oleyl alcohol, this combination do not form close film and results in poor emulsion.

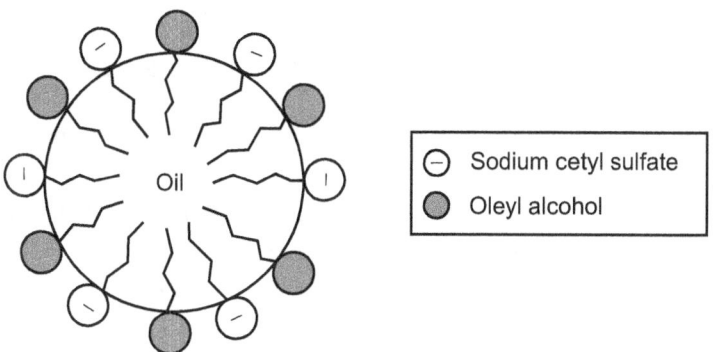

Fig. 3.9: Monomolecular film of sodium cetyl sulfate and oleyl alcohol showing poor emulsion with loose packing

Example 3: When cetyl alcohol is used with sodium oleate, this combination produce a close film but complexation is negligible, hence results in poor emulsion.

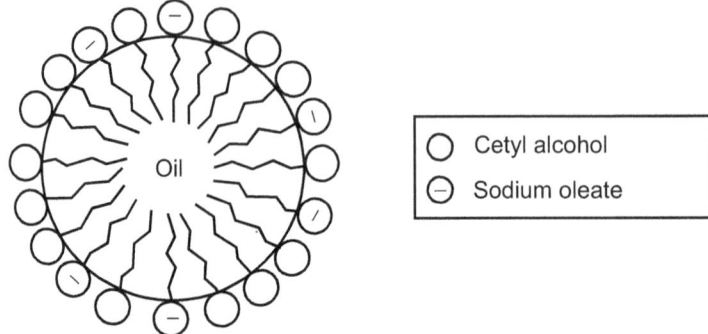

Fig. 3.10: Monomolecular film of sodium oleate and cetyl alcohol showing poor emulsion with close packing but negligible complexation

- The type of emulsion that is produced, oil in water or water in oil depends primarily on the property of the emulsifying agents. This characteristic is referred to as the hydrophile-lipophile balance (HLB), that is, the polar-non polar nature of the emulsifier.

- In general, o/w emulsions are formed when the HLB range of the emulsifier is within 9 to 12 and w/o emulsions are formed when the range is about 3 to 6.

- In the emulsifying agent such as sodium stearate, ($C_{17}H_{35}COONa$), $C_{17}H_{35}$ is the lipophilic, non-polar hydrocarbon chain or oil-loving group, whereas the carboxyl group, –COONa is the hydrophilic or polar, and lipophilic properties of emulsifier determines whether an oil in water or water in oil emulsion will result.

- An additional effect promoting stability is the presence of a surface charge which will cause repulsion between adjacent particles.

- The ability of combination of emulsifier to pack more tightly contributes to the overall strength of the film and hence, ultimately to the stability of the emulsion.

- Most emulsifiers probably form fairly dense gel structures at the interface and produce a stable interfacial film.

(II) Multi-molecular Film

- Multi-molecular adsorption is the mechanism of emulsifying agent by which coalescence can be prevented. The emulsifying agents like acacia and gelatin primarily tend to form a multimolecular film around the globules and secondarily reduces the interfacial tension. They are effective at high concentration.

- They also have affinity towards the oil phase and facilitate interfacial adsorption.

- They promote formation of oil-in-water type of emulsion.

- The stability can be improved by adding viscosity including agents such as tragacanth, methyl cellulose etc.

- The difference between surface active agents and hydrophilic colloids is that, the synthetic surface-active agents forms monomolecular film and later forms multimolecular film and also do not cause an appreciable lowering of interfacial tension.

(III) Solid Particle Film

- The finally divided solid particles that are wetted to some degree by both oil and water can act as emulsifying agents. These solid particles adsorb at oil-water interface and concentrated at the interface to form a rigid film of closely packed solids around the dispersed droplets so as to prevent coalescence. This solid film act as a mechanical barrier and prevent the coalescence of globules. These tend to produce coarse emulsion depending on affinity of emulsifier.
- Bentonite and Veegum follows solid particle adsorption.

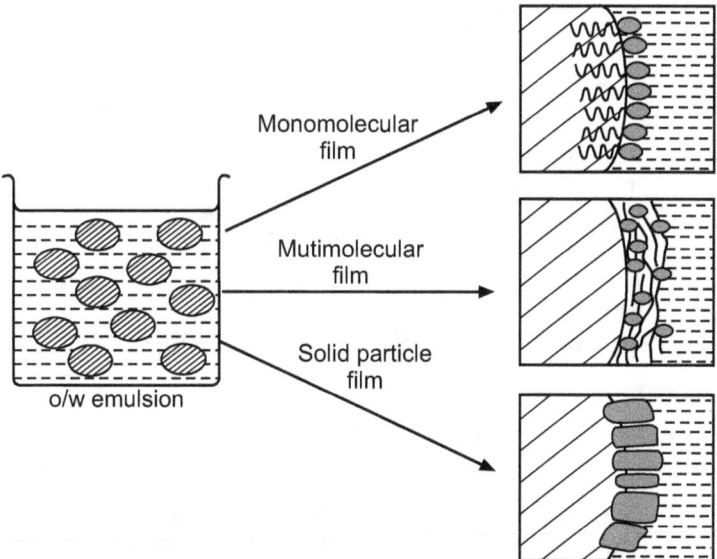

Fig. 3.11: Types of film formation

3.7 Emulsion Stabilization

- An emulsion can be stabilized by addition for suitable emulsifying agents.
- Interfacial tension between two phases decreases when surfactant adsorbs on the interface.
- The reduced interfacial tension depends on the concentration of the surfactant according to the Gibbs' isotherm. Adsorbed surfactants or solid particles stabilize emulsions via two main mechanisms:
  1. Electrostatic stabilization
  2. Steric stabilization
- Both electrostatic and steric forces can prevent aggregation or coalescence and hence stabilize emulsions.

1. **Electrostatic Stabilization:**
   - Repulsive forces are generated when electrical charged surfaces approach each other and then emulsion is stabilized which is called a 'Electrostatic Stabilization'. In an electrostatically stabilized emulsion, an ionic or ionisable surfactant forms a charged layer at the interface.

- For an oil-in-water emulsion, counter ions present in the continuous phase neutralize this layer. The charged surface and the counter ions are termed a double layer.
- If the counter ions are diffused (thick double layer), the disperse phase droplets act as charged spheres as they approach each other. If the repulsive forces are strong enough, the droplets are repelled before they can make contact and coalesce, and the emulsion is stable.
- In general, electrostatic stabilization is significant only for oil-in-water emulsions since the electric double-layer thickness is much greater in water than in oil.

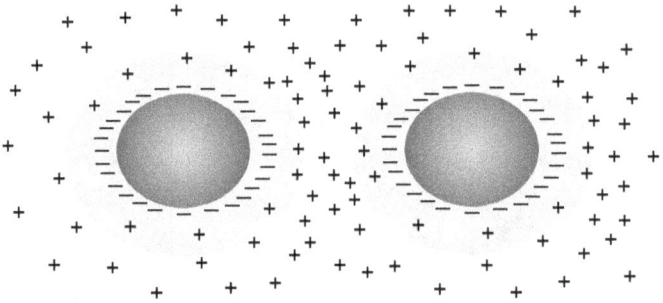

Fig. 3.12: Electrostatic stabilization

2. Steric Stabilization:

- Emulsions are made stable by steric stabilization which is a physical barrier to contact and coalescence. For example, high-molecular-weight polymers are adsorbed on the surface of the dispersed phase droplets and extend significantly into the continuous phase and provides a volume restriction or a physical barrier for particle interactions.
- As polymer coated/adsorbed particles approach, the repulsive forces arise, keeping particles apart from each other. The projections of emulsifying agents prevent coalescence of globules and act as a barrier. This phenomenon is a 'Steric Stabilization'.
- Surface-active solid particles such as clays have also been shown to sterically stabilize emulsions.

Fig. 3.13: Steric stabilization

3.8 Stability of Emulsions

- An emulsion is a thermodynamically unstable preparation, so care has to be taken that the chemical as well as the physical stability of the preparation remains intact throughout the shelf life. There should be no appreciable change in the mean particle size or the size distribution of the droplets of the dispersed phase and secondly droplets of the dispersed phase should remain uniformly distributed throughout the system.

- Instabilities seen in emulsion can be grouped as

  1. Creaming
  2. Cracking
  3. Phase inversion

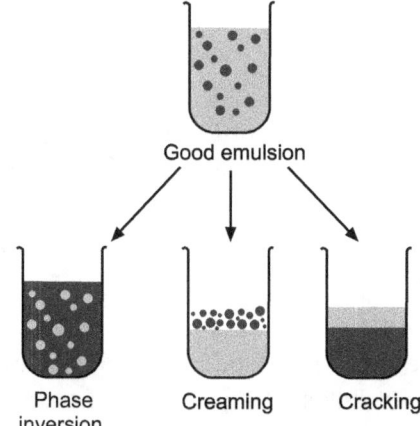

Fig. 3.14: Types instability of emulsion

1. Creaming:

- An emulsion is said to cream when the oil or fat rises to the surface, but remains in the form of globules, which may be redistributed throughout the dispersion medium by shaking.

- An oil of low viscosity tends to cream more readily than one of high viscosity. Increase in the viscosity of the medium decreases the tendency to cream.

- Creaming is a reversible phenomenon which can be corrected by mild shaking.

- The factors affecting creaming are best described by stroke's law:

$$V = \frac{d^2 (\rho_s - \rho_0)\, g}{18\, \eta}$$

Where,

V = rate of creaming

d = diameter of globules

ρ_s = density of dispersed phase

ρ_0 = density of dispersion medium

g = gravitational constant

η = viscosity of the dispersion medium

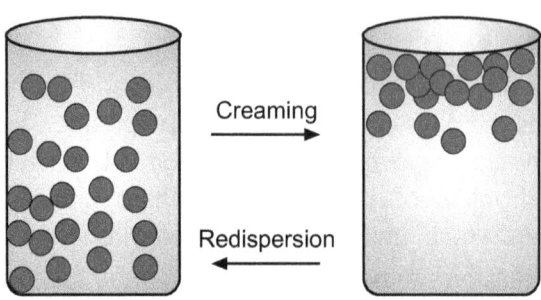

Fig. 3.15: Creaming of emulsions

The following approaches can be used for decreasing creaming

(i) Reduction of globule size: According to stroke's law, rate of creaming is directly proportional to the size of globules. Bigger is the size of the globules, more will be the creaming. Therefore in order to minimize creaming, globule size should be reduced by homogenization.

(ii) Increasing the viscosity of the continuous phase: Rate of creaming is inversely proportional to the viscosity of the continuous phase i.e. more the viscosity of the continuous phase, less will the problem of creaming. Therefore to avoid creaming in emulsions, the viscosity of the continuous phase should be increased by adding suitable viscosity enhancers like gum acacia, tragacanth etc.

(iii)Equalisation of density: To reduce the rate of creaming, the density difference between the dispersed phase and dispersed medium should be minimum. This can be achieved by addition of methyl cellulose, tragacanth and sodium alginate in to the aqueous external phase.

(iv) Storage temperature: The viscosity and solubility of an emulsifying agent is influenced by variation in storage temperature. At high temperature, due to reduction in viscosity, rate of creaming is greater. At refrigeration temperature, due to ice formation, deformation of oil globules under pressure of ice particles increases chances of coalescence. Hence an optimum temperature should be maintained.

2. Cracking or Coalescence:

*   Cracking involves coalescence of dispersed globules and separation of the dispersed phase as a separate layer. Thus two phase are distinctly separated in which redispersion can not be achieved even if shaking is done vigorously.

*   Reasons of cracking in emulsions might be either physical, chemical or biological effect that change the nature of interfacial film of an emulsifying agent and render it less stable to retain the process of emulsification of two immiscible liquid phases.

Cracking may takes place due to following reasons:

(i) Addition of an emulsifying agent of opposite type: Monovalent metal soap produces o/w emulsions while soap of divalent metal soap produces w/o emulsions; anionic and cationic emulsifying agents are mutually incompatible. Thus, avoid such incompatibilities.

(ii) **Decomposition or precipitaton of emulsifying agent:** Alkali soaps are decomposed by acids; sodium soaps are salted out by sodium chloride and certain other electrolytes; Anionic emulsifying agents are incompatible with substances having large cations and cationic emulsifying agents are incompatible with substances having large anions; Non-ionic emulsifying agents are incompatible with phenol; gums, proteins, gelatin and casein are insoluble in alcohol. So, one has to be careful about these incompatibilities to avoid cracking of emulsions.

(iii) **By addition of a common solvent:** The addition of a solvent to an emulsion, which is either miscible with or can dissolve the dispersed phase, the emulsifying agent and the continuous phase leads to the formation of one phase system or clear solution thus destroying the emulsion. For example, when alcohol is added to turpentine oil liniment it forms a clear solution because turpentine oil, soft soap and water get dissolved in alcohol.

(iv) **Microbial degradation:** The emulsions which are stored for a long time may develop bacterial and mould growth which may destroy the emulsifying agent and cause cracking. Therefore the emulsions which are not meant for immediate use must be suitably preserved.

(v) **Incorporation of excess disperse phase:** Chances of droplet collision are more in concentrated emulsion, which in turn increases probability of coalescence.

3. **Phase Inversion:**

- In phase inversion o/w type emulsion changes into w/o type and vice versa. It is a physical instability.

- It may be brought about by the addition of an electrolyte or by changing the phase volume ratio or by temperature changes.

- Phase inversion can be minimized by using the proper emulsifying agent in adequate concentration, keeping the concentration of dispersed phase between 30 to 60 % and by storing the emulsion in a cool place.

- On the other hand, Phase inversion refers to a phenomenon that occurs when oil-in-water emulsion is agitated; it reverts to water-in-oil and vice versa. Emulsification via phase inversion is widely used in fabrication of cosmetic products, pharmaceutical products (e.g., vesicles for drug delivery), foodstuff and detergents.

- Emulsification process is strongly affected by preparation method; very different droplet size distribution could be achieved, which is strictly linked to the product stability. Phase inversion process leads to the formation of finely dispersed droplets in a continuous phase.

3.9 The Hydrophilic-Lipophilic Balance (HLB) Scale

- In 1949, Griffin developed a system to assist making systematic decisions about the amount and types of emulsifying agents needed to form a stable emulsion. The system is called as the HLB (hydrophilic-lipophilic balance) system and has an arbitrary scale of 0 - 18.

- Each surfactant is allocated an HLB number representing the relative proportions of the lipophilic and hydrophilic groups in the molecules.
- A higher HLB number indicates that the emulsifier has a large number of hydrophilic groups in the molecules and therefore they are more hydrophilic in character.
- For example, Tweens have higher HLB numbers and they are also water soluble. Because of their water soluble character, tweens will cause the water phase to predominate and form an o/w emulsion.
- Surfactant having low HLB number indicates that the number of hydrophilic group present in the molecule is less and it has a lipophilic character.
- For example, spans generally have low HLB number and they are oil soluble. Because of their oil soluble character, spans cause the oil phase to predominate and form a w/o emulsion.

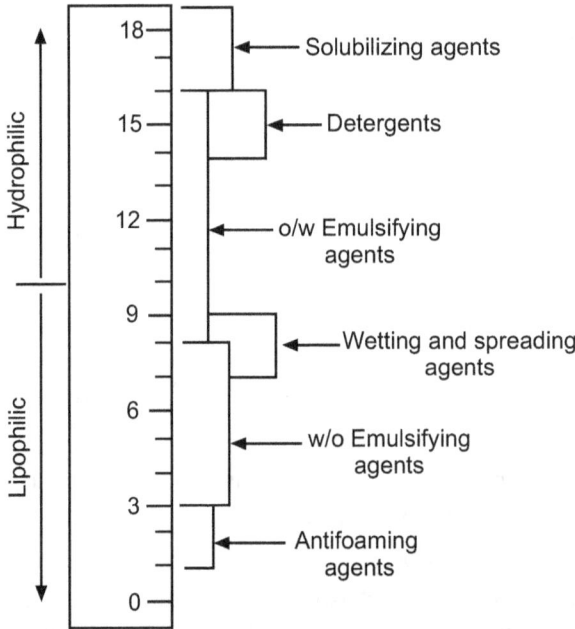

Fig. 3.16: HLB scale showing activity and HLB values of surfactants

Required HLB (RHLB):

- In HLB system, not only emulsifying agents have been assigned their HLB values but values also are assigned to oil and oil-substances.
- The concept of HLB in the preparation of a stable emulsion is that, HLB value of emulsifying agent(s) must be same as the HLB value of an oleaginous phase of an emulsion.
- For example, if one is preparing an emulsion of mineral oil, the HLB assigned to it in case w/o emulsion is 4 and in case of o/w is 10.5. Thus, stable emulsions are produced if the selected emulsifying agent possesses similar HLB values to the HLB values for mineral oil, depending on the type of emulsion desired.

- The combination of emulsifying agents have been utilized to achieve the proper HLB value for a particular emulsion.
- When a preparation contains more than one oil or wax, the 'required HLB' may be calculated by adding individual required HLB values.

Table 3.1: Required HLB values of oils and waxes

Material	For w/o	For o/w
Bees wax	5	12
Cetyl alcohol	-	15
Liquid paraffin	4	12
Soft paraffin	4	12
Wool fat	8	10

Example : Here, we will see one example to apply HLB-system in producing stable emulsions. Prepare a following emulsion, applying HLB-system.

Required HLB for first three substances are 12, 10 and 15 respectively, if o/w emulsion is prepared. Thus, total percentage of oil phase in the formula is, 40 + 2 + 1 = 43. Now, we have to find out the proportions of the oil phase out of total oil phase.

Liquid paraffin	40 %
Wool fat	2 %
Cetyl alcohol	1 %
Emulgent	8 %
Water	q. s. to produce 100 %

$$\text{Liquid paraffin:} \frac{40}{43} \times 100 = 93\ \%$$

$$\text{Wool fat:} \frac{2}{43} \times 100 = 4.7\ \%$$

$$\text{Cetyl alcohol:} \frac{1}{43} \times 100 = 2.3\ \%$$

Total required HLB value is obtained as follows :

(1) Individual HLB for liquid paraffin $= \frac{93}{100} \times 12 = 11.16$

(2) Individual HLB for wool fat $= \frac{4.7}{100} \times 10 = 0.47$

(3) Individual HLB for cetyl alcohol $= \frac{2.3}{100} \times 15 = 0.35$

Thus, the total required HLB for the system

$$= 11.16 + 0.47 + 0.35$$
$$= 11.98$$

Now, to obtain HLB value equal to 11.98, we have to select the emulsifying agent or agents, e.g. two emulsifying agents in combination can be added to supply this particular value i.e. Span 80, which has HLB = 4.3; and Tween 80, which has HLB = 15.

The amount of span 80 and tween 80 based on the RHLB of liquid paraffin can be calculated by allegation method as shown below.

Span 80 (4.3)   (15 – 11.98) = 3.02 parts of span 80

$\qquad\qquad$ 11.98

Tween 80 (15)   (11.98 – 4.7) = 7.68 parts of Tween 80

$$\text{Total} = 10.7 \text{ parts}$$

$$\text{Quantity of Span 80} = \frac{3.02}{10.7} \times 8 = 2.26 \text{ g}$$

$$\text{Quantity of Tween 80} = \frac{7.68}{10.7} \times 8 = 5.74 \text{ g}$$

Thus 2.26 g of Span 80 and 5.74 g of Tween 80 are required to produce a stable o/w emulsion.

So this example reveals that HLB-system is useful in practice.

3.10 Phase Inversion Temperature

- The temperature at which the inversion occurs depends on emulsifier concentration and is called *phase inversion temperature* (PIT). Temperature affects the stability of emulsion. The most important influence that temperature has on an emulsion is probably inversion.

- Almost 50 years ago it was observed that w/o emulsions of benzene in water that were stabilized with sodium stearate invert to o/w emulsions when heated and reform w/o emulsions when cooled.

- When emulsions are prepared at relatively high temperatures and allow to cool at room temperature then this type of inversion is likely to happen. Emulsions formed by a phase inversion technique are generally considered quite stable and are believed to contain a finely dispersed internal phase.

- The PIT is generally considered to be the temperature at which the *hydrophilic* and the *lipophilic* properties of the emulsifier are in *balance* and is therefore also called the HLB temperature.

- Shinoda's description of the processes at or near the PIT is almost universally accepted today. An o/w emulsion stabilized by a non-ionic polyoxyethylene-derived surfactant contains oil-swollen micelles of the surfactant as well as emulsified oil. When the temperature is raised, the water-solubility of the surfactant decreases; as a result, the micelles are broken, and the size of emulsified oil droplets begins to increase.

- A continued rise in the temperature causes separation into an oil phase, a surfactant phase and water. It is near this temperature that the water-insoluble surfactant begins to form a w/o emulsion containing both water-swollen micelles and emulsified water droplets in a continuous oil phase.

3.11 Krafft Point and Cloud Point

Krafft Point:

- Solubility of surfactant depends on the temperature of system. At low temperatures a saturated surfactant solution will be in equilibrium with solid surfactant; the temperature is too low for micelles to form and the limiting solubility will be low.

- **At the Krafft temperature** it becomes possible to form micelles and the surfactant becomes much more soluble; there is a break in the solubility curve, as shown in Fig. 1.20, example is sodium decylsulphonate.

- **Below krafft point:** No formation of micelle, and limited solubility of surfactant.

- **Above krafft point:** Formation of micelles, and the surfactant become much more soluble.

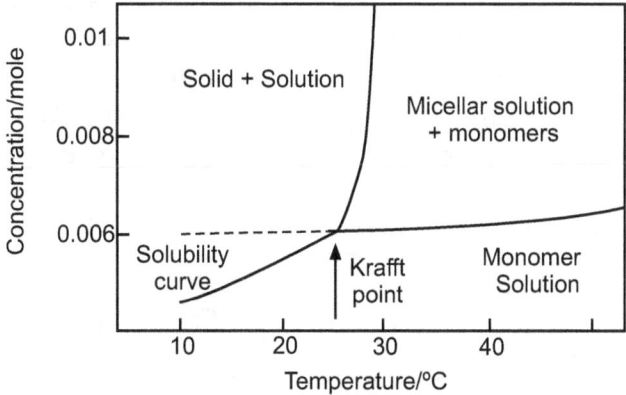

Fig. 3.17: Krafft point of surfactant

- The CMC is primarily determined by the hydrophobic group of surfactant.

  The Krafft temperature depends strongly on;

  1. The nature of the head group and
  2. The length of the hydrocarbon chain.

- The hydrocarbon fragments have to be in a liquid state for micelle formation to occur. Solidification of the hydrocarbon chain is favoured by the cohesion between hydrocarbon chains, which increases with their length. Thus, the Krafft temperature increases with chain length, as shown for the Krafft temperatures of the sulphonates in the Table 3.2.

Table 3.2: Krafft temperatures of the sulphonates

$C_{10}SO_3Na$	$C_{12}SO_3Na$	$C_{14}SO_3Na$	$C_{16}SO_3Na$	$C_{18}SO_3Na$
22°C	34°C	43°C	52°C	60°C

Cloud Point:

- **Cloud point** is the temperature above which an aqueous solution of a water-soluble surfactant becomes turbid. (Fig. 3.18)

- Knowing the cloud point is important for:

    1. Determining storage stability. Storing formulations at temperatures significantly higher than the cloud point may result in phase separation and instability.
    2. Wetting, cleaning and foaming characteristics can be different above and below the cloud point.
    3. Generally, non-ionic surfactants show optimal effectiveness when used near or below their cloud point.
    4. Low-foam surfactants should be used at temperatures slightly above their cloud point.

- Cloud points are typically measured using 1% aqueous surfactant solutions. Cloud points range from 0° to 100°C (32 to 212°F), limited by the freezing and boiling points of water.

- Cloud points are characteristic of non-ionic surfactants. Anionic surfactants (with negatively charged groups) are more water-soluble than non-ionic surfactants and will typically have much higher cloud points (above 100°C). The presence of other components in a formulation can depress or increase the solution's cloud point. For example, the addition of a coupler or hydrotrope can increase the cloud point of a solution, whereas builders or other salts will depress the cloud point temperature.

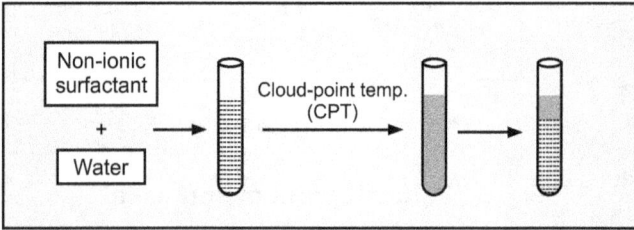

Fig. 3.18: Cloud points

3.12 Formulation of Emulsion

An emulsion consist of

1. Drug
2. Oil phase
3. Aqueous phase
4. Emulsifying agents
5. Antioxidants
6. Preservatives

7. Organoleptic additives
8. Buffering agents
9. Hamectants
10. Density modifiers

1. Drug:

- In emulsions, drug component is either soluble in oil phase (oil soluble vitamins) or in aqueous phase or sometimes oil phase is itself act as the drug component such as castor oil and liquid paraffin.

2. Oil Phase:

- Oil phase plays various roles in an emulsion. Oil phase may act as a drug, e.g. Turpentine oil as a counter irritant, castor oil and liquid paraffin as a laxative.
- Oil phase may be used to dissolve oil soluble drugs. Oil phase may be used as emollient and lubricant.
- Oily phase which varies in consistency, is used to adjust consistency of final product.
- Oily phase may used for *in-situ* soap formation e.g. Oleic acid in white liniment and in oily calamine lotion.

3. Aqueous Phase:

- Freshly boiled and cooled water is used as an aqueous phase for emulsion.
- However in some emulsions aromatic waters have been used as an aqueous phase.
- Lime water is also used for *in-situ* soap formation in oily calamine lotion.
- When the drugs or ingredients are soluble in aqueous phase then they are first dissolved in the aqueous phase and then mixed with the oil phase.

4. Emulsifying Agents:

- **Emulsifying agent are the substances which reduce the interfacial tension between the two immiscible liquids.** They adsorb on the surface of the dispersed phase of an emulsion. Emulsifying agents are also called as **emulgents** or **emulsifiers**.

Classification of Emulsifying Agents:

According to physicochemical nature emulsifying agents are classified as follows:

(I) Polysaccharides:

(i) Natural polysaccharides:

(a) Acacia
(b) Tragacanth
(c) Agar
(d) Pectin

(ii) Semi-synthetic polysaccharides:

   (a) Methyl cellulose

   (b) Sodium carboxymethyl cellulose

(II) Surfactants:

   (a) Anionic

   (b) Cationic

   (c) Non-ionic

   (d) Amphoteric

(III) Finely divided solids:

   (a) Bentonite

   (b) Milk of magnesia

   (c) Magnesium trisilicate

   (d) Magnesium aluminium silicate

   (e) Magnesium oxide

(IV) Sterol containing substances:

   (a) Beeswax

   (b) Wool fat

   (c) Wool alcohol

These are explained below :

(I) Polysaccharides:

(i) Natural polysaccharides:

- These hydrocolloids are o/w emulsifying agent. They act by forming multi-molecular interfacial film and by increasing viscosity of water phase. Some of them act as true emulsifiers which are also known as primary emulsifying agents while others act as emulsion stabilizers also known as secondary emulsifying agents.

- They are capable of emulsifying a large number of substances but the resulting emulsions will have to be preserved by adding a suitable preservative because the polysaccharides act as very good medium for bacterial growth. The preservatives which can be added are sodium benzoate, benzoic acid or a combination of methyl paraben and propyl paraben.

(a) **Acacia:** Acacia is the most popularly used natural emulsifying agent for oral emulsions. It is generally used in the concentration of 8 - 15% and gives a stable and palatable emulsion over the pH range of 2 - 10. Emulsions tend to cream using acacia as the viscosity is low.

(b) **Tragacanth:** Tragacanth alone is rarely used because it does not reduce interfacial tension and it forms thick and coarse emulsions. Tragacanth is used as emulsion stabilizer in the ratio of 1 part to 10 parts of acacia.

(c) Agar: Agar is commonly used as thickening agent along with acacia in the concentration of 2%.

(d) Pectin: Pectin is a purified complex carbohydrate obtained from inner rind of citrus fruit and from the pulp of apple and guava. It acts as emulsion stabilizer in acacia emulsion.

(ii) Semi-synthetic polysaccharides:

- Includes mainly cellulose derivatives like sodium carboxy methyl cellulose, methyl cellulose. They are used for formulating o/w type of emulsions. They are non-toxic, and are less subject to microbial growth. They primarily act by increasing the viscosity of the system.

(a) Methyl cellulose: Methyl cellulose is widely used in the pharmaceutical industry as suspending, thickening and emulsifying agent. This is non-ionic in nature and is stable over a wide pH range. It is mainly used for emulsification of mineral and vegetables oil. Drawback of methyl cellulose is that it gets precipitated in the presence of large quantities of electrolytes.

(b) Sodium carboxymethyl cellulose: It is anionic in nature. It is not acting as an true emulsifier but is used as emulsion stabilizer the concentration of 0.5 to 1.0%

(II) Surfactants:

- They are prepared synthetically and are superior to other types of emulsifying agent usually of natural origin since they are not susceptible to decomposition by microorganisms.

- This group contains surface active agents which act by getting adsorbed at the oil water interface in such a way that the hydrophilic polar groups are oriented towards water and lipophillic non-polar groups are oriented towards oil, thus forming a stable film. This film acts as a mechanical barrier and prevents coalescence of the globules of the dispersed phase.

- They are classified according to the ionic charge possessed by the molecules of the surfactant e.g., anionic, cationic, non-ionic and amphoteric.

(a) Anionic surfactants: The long anion chain on dissociation imparts surface activity, while the cation is inactive. These agents are primarily used for external preparations and not for internal use as they have an unpleasant bitter taste and irritant action on the intestinal mucosa. e.g., alkali soaps, amine soaps, divalent metallic soaps, alkyl sulphates and phosphates.

Alkali soaps: Produce good oil in water emulsions. They are unstable at pH below 10 and are incompatible with acids and polyvalent inorganic and long chain organic cations.

e.g. Sodium oleate, Sodium stearate.

Amine soaps: Amine soaps are formed *in situ* during emulsification by interaction of long chain fatty acid with an organic base such as triethanol amine, morpholine.

Amine soaps produce o/w emulsions at about pH 8. They unstable towards acids and polyvalent cations. e.g. Triethanolamine oleate, Triethanolamine stearate.

Divalent Metallic Soaps: Calcium salts of fatty acids are generally used for formulating w/o emulsion. Metallic soaps are incompatible with monovalent emulsifying agents.

e.g. Calcium oleate.

Alkyl Sulphates and Phosphates: They produce stable o/w emulsions when used in combination with fatty alcohols.

e.g. Sodium lauryl sulphate (SLS).

(b) **Cationic surfactants:** The positive charge cations produced on dissociation are responsible for emulsifying properties.

They are mainly used in external preparations such as lotions and creams. These compounds besides having good antibacterial activity are also used in combination with secondary emulsifying agents to produce o/w emulsions for external application.

They are incompatible with anionic emulsifying agents.

e.g. Quaternary ammonium compounds such as cetrimide, benzalkonium chloride and benzethonium chloride.

(c) **Non-ionic surfactants:** They are the class of surfactants widely used as emulsifying agents. They are extensively used to produce both oil-in-water and water-in-oil emulsions for internal as well as external use.

The emulsions prepared using these surfactants remain stable over a wide range of pH changes and are not affected by the addition of acids and electrolytes.

They also show low irritancy as compared to other surfactants.

E.g. glyceryl esters such as glyceryl monostearate, propylene glycol monostearate, macrogol esters such as polyoxyl stearates, sorbitan fatty acid esters such as spans and their polyoxyethylene derivatives such as tweens (polysorbates).

(d) **Amphoteric surfactants:** These are the substances whose ionic charge depends on the pH of the system. Below a certain pH, these are cationic while above a defined pH, these are cationic. At intermediate pH these behave as zwitterions. e.g. lecithin.

(III) Finely Divided Solids:

- Several inorganic substances such as bentonite, milk of magnesia, magnesium trisilicate, colloidal anhydrous silica, magnesium aluminium silicate, magnesium oxide, hectorite etc. are used in the preparation of pharmaceutical emulsion.

- This group consists of finely divided solids having balanced hydrophilic lipophillic properties. They accumulate at the oil/water interface and form a coherent interfacial film around the droplets of dispersed phase globules and prevent coalescence.

- The emulsions formed using finely divided solids are stable and less prone to microbial contamination.

(IV) Sterol Containing Substances:

- Beeswax, wool fat, wool alcohols are w/o type of emulsifying agents, but in most cases these are used as emulsion stabilizers.
- Beeswax is used with borax to form sodium cerotate which is an emulsifying agent in cold cream.
- Wool fat is also known as *anhydrous lanolin*. Wool fat is practically insoluble in water but can absorb 50% of its weight of water and produces w/o type of emulsion.
- Wool alcohol is nothing but emulsifying fraction of wool fat, used as w/o emulsion stabilizer and as emollient.

Criteria for the selection of emulsifying agents:

An ideal emulsifying agent should posses the following characteristics:

1. It should be able to reduce the interfacial tension between the two immiscible liquids.
2. It should be physically and chemically stable, inert and compatible with the other ingredients of the formulation.
3. It should be completely non-irritant and non-toxic in the concentrations used.
4. It should be organoleptically inert i.e. should not impart any colour, odour or taste to the preparation.
5. It should be able to form a coherent film around the globules of the dispersed phase and should prevent the coalescence of the droplets of the dispersed phase.
6. It should be able to produce and maintain the required viscosity of the preparation.

The choice of selection of emulsifying agent plays a very important role in the formulation of a stable emulsion. No single emulsifying agent possesses all the properties required for the formulation of a stable emulsion therefore sometimes blends of emulsifying agents have to be taken.

5. Antioxidants:

- Rancidity is the major problem associated with emulsion containing unsaturated fats and oils. To prevent this, antioxidants are incorporated in emulsions.
- Choice of particular antioxidant depends on its safety, efficacy and acceptability for particular use.
- Antioxidants are commonly used at concentration ranging from 0.001 to 0.1%.
- Oil soluble antioxidants such as BHA (Butylated Hydroxy Anisole) and BHT (Butylated Hydroxy Toluene), propyl gallate, L-tocopherol, while some water soluble antioxidants like ascorbic acid, citric acid, tartaric acid, sodium metabisulphite are popularly used in emulsion.

6. Preservatives:

- In emulsion the aqueous phase is more sensitive to microbial growth and hence preservatives added in an emulsion, must be present in the aqueous phase in sufficient concentration to prevent the microbial growth.

- Preservatives should remain in its unionized form and should have oil-water partition coefficient less than one.
- e.g. glutareldehyde, benzoic acid, sorbic acid, benzalkonium chloride and benzethonium chloride, methyl, ethyl, propyl and butyl esters of p-hydroxybenzoic acid etc.

7. Organoleptic Additives:
- Sweetening agents are used to impart sweetness to emulsions for oral use. e.g. Aspartame, sodium saccharin, sucrose, sorbitol etc.
- Flavouring agents are used in the emulsions to mask the unpleasant taste of oil. e.g. lemon oil, peppermint oil etc.
- Pharmaceutical emulsions have acceptable milky appearance hence colouring agents are not needed in an emulsion.

8. Buffering Agents:
- The addition of buffers in emulsion may be necessary to maintain chemical stability of the drug or to control tonicity or to ensure physiological compatibility.
- The choice of suitable buffer depends on the pH and buffering capacity required.
- e.g. citrate, phosphate, acetate etc.

9. Humectants:
- Humectants are added to emulsion formulation in order to reduce the evaporation of the water either from the surface of the skin after application or from the packaged product when the closure is removed.
- e.g. Glycerol, polyethylene glycol, propylene glycol etc.

10. Density Modifiers:
- From Stoke's Law, it can be seen that if the disperse phase and continuous phases both have the same densities, then creaming will not occur.
- Minor modifications in density, by adding sucrose, glycerol or propylene glycol can be achieved.

3.13 Methods for Preparing Emulsions

- Preparation of emulsions depends on the scale at which it is produced. On small scale mortar and pestle can be used, but its efficiency is limited. To overcome these drawbacks small electric mixers can be used although care must be exercised to avoid excessive entrapment of air. For large scale production, mechanical stirrers are used to provide controlled agitation and shearing stress to produce stable emulsions.
- The methods commonly used to prepare emulsions on laboratory scale are as follows:

1. Dry Gum Method (Continental Method):
In this method, the oil is first triturated with gum with a little amount of water to form the primary emulsion. The trituration is continued till a characteristic 'clicking' sound is heard and a thick white cream is formed. Once the primary emulsion is formed, the remaining quantity of water is slowly added to form the final emulsion.

2. Wet Gum Method (English Method):

As the name implies, in this method first gum and water are triturated together to form a mucilage. The required quantity of oil is then added gradually in small proportions with thorough trituration to form the primary emulsion. Once the primary emulsion has been formed, remaining quantity of water is added to make the final emulsion.

3. Bottle Method:

This method is employed for preparing emulsions containing volatile and other non-viscous oils. Both dry gum and wet gum methods can be employed for the preparation. As volatile oils have a low viscosity as compared to fixed oils, they require comparatively large quantity of gum for emulsification. In this method, oil or water is first shaken thoroughly and vigorously with the calculated amount of gum. Once this has emulsified completely, the second liquid (either oil or water) is then added all at once and the bottle is again shaken vigorously to form the primary emulsion. More of water is added in small portions with constant agitation after each addition to produce the final volume.

Table 3.3: Proportions of Oil, Water and Gum required for formation of primary emulsion

Type of oil	Proportions of		
	Oil	Water	Gum
Fixed oil	4	2	1
Mineral oil	3	2	1
Volatile oil	2	2	1

4. In-situ Soap Method:

In this method, the emulsifying agent (soap) is not externally added but it is formed while preparing the emulsion.

Soap is formed by mixing equal volumes of oil and an aqueous solution containing a sufficient amount of alkali.

Two types of soaps formed *in-situ* in this method are monovalent soap (soft soap) and divalent soap.

This method is suitable for the formation of an o/w or w/o emulsion. It depend upon the nature of soap formed. If the soap formed is monovalent then o/w emulsion is formed and if soap formed is divalent then w/o emulsion is formed.

Some Examples of Emulsions:

Example 1: Liquid Paraffin Emulsion I.P.

Formula :

Liquid Paraffin	50 ml
Indian Gum	12.5 gm
Sodium Benzoate	0.5 gm
Tragacanth	0.5 gm

Vanillin	0.05 gm
Glycerin	12.5 gm
Chloroform	0.25ml
Freshly boiled and cooled water q.s. to make	100 ml

Liquid paraffin is a hydrocarbon base, which is been used for its laxative activity. It softens stools and facilitates effective lubrication.

Indian Gum is an emulsifying agent where Tragacanth and Glycerine is added to increase the viscosity. Tragacanth is added with Indian Gum to stabilize the emulsion and to increase the viscosity of aqueous phase. Chloroform enhances dispersion of gums. Sodium benzoate is added to preserve the emulsion as it contains water and flavour is Vanillin to add, overall acceptability to the formulation.

Procedure:

1. Emulsion is prepared by dry gum method.
2. Prepare Primary emulsion- For this, liquid paraffin and chloroform is triturated with the gum, tragacanth and vanillin. Add ¼th vehicle and triturate to produce creamy primary emulsion.
3. Mix sodium benzoate in small quantity of vehicle.
4. Add sodium benzoate solution and glycerin to primary emulsion.
5. Triturate uniformly and adjust the final volume with remaining quantity of vehicle.
6. Transfer emulsion to a suitable amber coloured glass bottle, label and dispence.
7. Label as:
    FOR INTERNAL USE ONLY.
    SHAKE WELL BEFORE USE.
    DO NOT FREEZE.
    STORE IN COOL AND DRY PLACE.
    REPALCE CAP TIGHTLY AFTER USE.

Category: Laxative

Example 2: Terpentine Liniment I.P.

Formula:

Soft Soap	9.0 gm
Camphor	5.0 gm
Turpentine Oil	65.0 ml
Freshly boiled and cooled water q.s. to make	100 ml

This formulation is used for the treatment of pains associated with joints, muscles and tendons. Camphor and turpentine oil are counter irritants and rubefacients as well. Turpentine oil is a volatile oil. Soft soap is a monovelent soap, it is a hydrophilic emulsifying agent. It has surface activity and thus increases skin penetration.

Procedure:

1. First dissolve the camphor in turpentine oil and keep it aside.
2. Prepare mixture of soft soap and small quantity of water.
3. Now, mix well above two mixtures and transfer to tared bottle with little quantity of water and shake thoroughly to get creamy emulsion.
4. Adjust the final volume with remaining quantity of vehicle.
5. Transfer emulsion to a suitable amber coloured glass bottle, label and dispence.
6. Label as:

   FOR EXTERNAL USE ONLY.

   APPLY WITH FRICTION ON INTACT SKIN.

   SHAKE WELL BEFORE USE.

   DO NOT FREEZE.

   STORE IN COOL AND DRY PLACE.

   REPALCE CAP TIGHTLY AFTER USE.

Category : Counter Irritants and Rubefacient

Example 3: Castor Oil Emulsion

Formula:

Castor Oil	8 ml
Acacia powder	2 gm
Water (freshly boiled and cooled) q.s. to make	30 ml

Castor oil is used as laxative for evacuation of bowel in constipation. Acacia is natural emulsifying agent.

Procedure:

1. Emulsion is prepared by Wet gum method.
2. Take acacia in a morter.
3. Add small portions of water and triturate.
4. Then add castor oil in a small portion and triturate rapidly until a clicking sound is produced and the product become white or nearly white.
5. Add more water in small portions to produce final volume.
6. Transfer emulsion to a suitable colurless glass bottle, label and dispence.
7. Label as:

   FOR INTERNAL USE ONLY.

   SHAKE WELL BEFORE USE.

   DO NOT FREEZE.

   STORE IN COOL AND DRY PLACE.

   REPALCE CAP TIGHTLY AFTER USE.

Category: Laxative

3.14 Multiple Emulsions

- Multiple emulsions are also known as, emulsions of emulsions, liquid membrane system or double emulsion. There are two major types of multiple emulsions that are the w/o/w and o/w/o double emulsions. But w/o/w type of emulsion is the most common multiple emulsion widely used for pharmaceutical purposes.

  This is complex liquid dispersion system. In this, the droplets of one dispersed liquid (water-in-oil or oil-in-water) are further dispersed in another liquid i.e. water or oil respectively resulting into w/o/w or o/w/o multiple emulsions.

3.14.1 Types of Multiple Emulsions

The two major types of multiple emulsions are the water-oil-water (w/o/w) and oil-water-oil (o/w/o) double emulsions.

Water-in-Oil-in-Water (w/o/w) Emulsion System"

- In W/O/W system, an organic phase (hydrophobic) separates internal and external aqueous phase. In other words, w/o/w is a system in which oil droplets may be surrounded by an aqueous phase, which in turn encloses one or several water droplets.

Oil-in-Water-in-Oil (o/w/o) Emulsion System:

- In o/w/o systems, an aqueous phase (hydrophilic) separates internal and external oil phase. In other words, o/w/o is a system in which water droplets may be surrounded in oil phase, which in turn encloses one or more oil droplets.

3.14.2 Uses of Multiple Emulsions

1. It gives prolonged action.
2. It is used for Taste masking.
3. It improves stability.
4. It is a more effective dosage form.
5. It protects drug against external environment.
6. Used in enzyme entrapment.

3.14.3 Formulation of Multiple Emulsions

Oil Phase:

- The oil phase to be employed in a pharmaceutical emulsion must be non-toxic. The various oils of vegetable origin such as soybean, sesame, peanut, safflower, olive, Jojoba, arachis etc. are acceptable if purified correctly. Refined hydrocarbons such as light liquid paraffin, squalane, as well as esters of fatty acids including ethyl oleate and isopropyl myristate have also been used in double emulsions.

- Oils derived from vegetable sources are biodegradable, whereas those based on mineral oils are only removed very slowly from the body.

- As a general rule, multiple emulsions (w/o/w) produced from mineral oils are more stable than those produced from vegetable oils.

- The order of decreasing stability and percentage entrapment has been found to be light liquid paraffin > squalane > sesame oil > maize or peanut oil.

Nature and Quantity of Emulsifying Agents:

- At least two surfactants of different nature i.e. one hydrophilic and another lipophilic are required for the preparation of 'Multiple Emulsion', as primary and secondary emulsifiers depending upon the type of emulsion to be prepared.

- Mostly the mixtures of non-ionic surfactants are used at various concentrations to obtain stable systems. These emulsifiers are preferred because of their low toxicity and their interaction with other compounds is expected to be less. The concentration of the emulsifiers can also be varied. Too little emulsifier may result in unstable systems, whereas too much emulsifier may lead to toxic effects and can even cause destabilization.

- The optimum concentration of surfactant used to emulsify the given oil is determined using hydrophile-lipophile balance (HLB) systems. In general, for a w/o/w emulsion the optimal HLB value will be in the range 2 - 7 for the primary surfactant and in the range 6 - 16 for the secondary surfactant.

- The inversion of w/o/w emulsion to simple o/w emulsion may occur due to excess of lipophilic surfactant.

- Surfactants are generally sorbitan mono oleate, sorbitan mono laurate, sorbitan sesquioleate, polyoxyethylene sorbitan mono oleate, polyoxyethylene sorbitan mono laurate, polyoxyethylene sorbitan monosesquioleate, and polyoxyethylene octadecyl ethers etc. are used.

3.14.5 Phase Volume

- It is very important to have proper order of phase addition while formulation, and dispersed phase should be added slowly into the continuous phase for the formulation of a stable multiple emulsion. An optimal (22 - 50%) internal phase volume can be utilized for the emulsion formulation. Very high phase volume ratio (70 - 90%) had also been reported to produce a stable multiple emulsion.

3.14.6 Methods of Preparation

1. Two-Step Emulsification Method (Double Emulsification):

- This is very easy and most common method. It gives high yield with reproducibility.

- It is a double emulsification process in which primary emulsion is re-emulsified to get multiple emulsions. In this method, two stages are involved.

    (i) Preparation of ordinary w/o or o/w primary emulsion by using appropriate emulsifier system.

    (ii) Then reemulsification of freshly prepared w/o or o/w primary emulsion is with an excess of aqueous phase or oil phase. The final prepared emulsion could be w/o/w or o/w/o respectively.

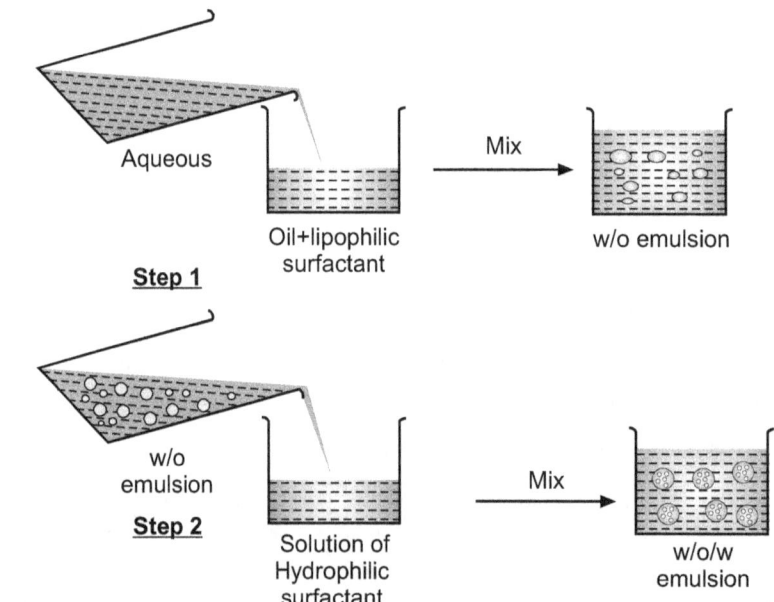

Fig. 3.19: Two-step emulsification method

2. Modified Two-Step Emulsification Technique:

- This method is different from the conventional two-step technique in two points:

    (i) In this fine, homogenous and stable w/o emulsion was obtained by Sonication and stirring.

    (ii) A continuous phase is poured into a dispersed phase for preparing w/o/w emulsion. Moreover, 1 : 4 : 5 ratio is fixed for the composition of internal aqueous phase : oily phase : external phase which produce most stable formulation as reported for most of w/o/w emulsions.

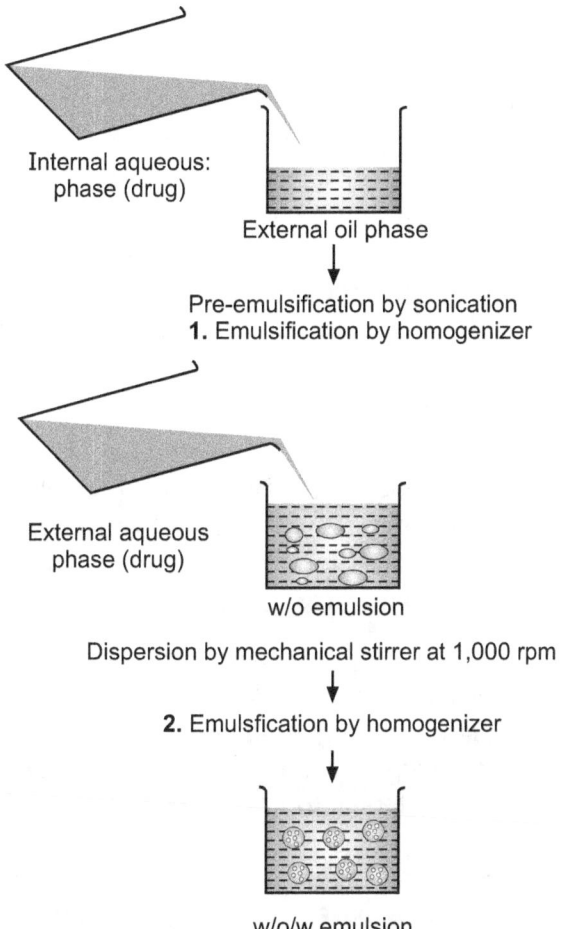

Fig. 3.20: Modified two-step emulsification technique

3. Phase Inversion Technique (One Step Method):

- When concentration of dispersed globules in dispersion medium is quite high that leads to phase inversion of emulsion. The concentrated o/w emulsion is thermally induced to produce w/o/w emulsion. The w/o/w emulsion is obtained due to phase inversion of w/o emulsion, when an aqueous solution of hydrophilic emulsifier is introduced into oil containing lipophilic surfactant.

- An **emulsified microemulsion technique** has also been utilized to prepare multiple emulsions in a single step. In this process, oil phase is dispersed within water by surfactant to produce w/o microemulsion, then emulsify this with water to yield o/w/o multiple emulsion.

4. Membrane Emulsification Technique:

- A special apparatus consisting of two chambers, upper and lower is used for emulsification. Between these two chambers a Porous Glass Membrane is fitted as a means of emulsification.

- In this primary emulsion, w/o or o/w is formed by sonication and it is filled into the upper chamber. Lower chamber contains final external phase or it is feeded with continuously with final external phase.

- A primary emulsion (dispersed phase) is then extruded into an external phase (a continuous phase) under a constant pressure through a Porous Glass Membrane, which should have controlled and homogenous pores. Nitrogen gas fed into the upper chamber initiates the permeation of the primary emulsion through the controlled-pore of glass membrane into the lower chamber, generating the multiple globules. The particle size of the multiple emulsion can be controlled with the proper selection of porous glass membrane.

5. **Micro Channel Emulsification:**
    - The emulsion was prepared by first homogenizing a mixture of water and oil phase through conventional homogenizer. This primary emulsion w/o is then forced through the micro-channel device into a second continuous phase i.e. water, which must contain a suitable emulsifier for oil phase stabilization.

3.14.7 Applications of Multiple Emulsions

1. **Taste Masking:** Taste masking of chlorpromazine, an antipsychotic drug and chloroquine, an antimalarial agent has also been reported by multiple emulsions.

2. **Controlled and Sustained Drug Delivery:** In both systems drug present in innermost phase has to cross several phases before it is available for absorption for the system. Hence it has potential to act as Controlled and Sustained Drug Delivery system.

3. **Bioavailability Enhancer:** The lipophilic drugs, which have high first pass metabolism for those multiple emulsions have been used to improve bioavailability. Multiple emulsion increases bioavailability of drugs either by protecting drugs in physiological, ionic/enzymatic environment in the GIT where otherwise these gets degraded like proteins, peptides or by passing the hepatic first pass metabolism.

4. **As a Immuno-adjuvant:** Standard w/o emulsions are used as vaccine adjuvants but due to viscous nature they are difficult to inject. The re-emulsification of w/o emulsion to w/o/w emulsion gives consistency enough for administration.

5. **In Cosmetology:** Various cosmetic preparations such as sun creams, shaving creams, hand creams, make-up cleansers, antiperspirants have been prepared by incorporating the active ingredient either in internal or external phases. They are easy to apply and make skin healthy.

3.15 Microemulsions

- Microemulsions are clear, transparent, thermodynamically stable dispersions of oil and water, stabilized by an interfacial film of surfactant frequently in combination with a co-surfactant.

- Alternative names for these systems are often used, such as swollen micelle, transparentemulsion, solubilized oil and micellar solution.

Advantages of Microemulsion System:

1. Microemulsions are easily prepared and require no energy contribution during preparation this is due to better thermodynamic stability.

2. The formation of microemulsion is reversible. They may become unstable at low or high temperature but when the temperature returns to the stability range, the microemulsion reforms.

3. Microemulsions are thermodynamically stable system and allows self-emulsification of the system.

4. Microemulsions have low viscosity compared to emulsions.

5. Microemulsions provide improved drug solubilization and bioavailability.

6. The use of microemulsion as delivery system can improve the efficacy of a drug, allowing the total dose to be reduced and thus minimizing side effects.

Disadvantages of Microemulsion System:

1. Microemulsion system have limited solubilizing capacity for high melting substances.

2. Require large amount of surfactants for stabilizing droplets.

3. Microemulsion stability is influenced by environmental parameters such as temperature and pH.

Table 3.4: Basic difference between macroemulsion and microemulsion

Macroemulsion	Microemulsion
1. They are lyophobic in nature.	1. They are the border between lyophilic and lyophobic.
2. Droplet diameter 1 to 20 mm.	2. Droplet diameter 10 to 100 mm.
3. Macroemulsion droplets exist as individual entities.	3. Microemulsion droplets disappear within fraction of seconds.
4. Emulsion droplets are roughly spherical droplets of one phase dispersed into the other phase.	4. Microemulsions are the structures of various droplets like bi-continuous to swollen micelles.
5. Macroemulsions requires quick agitation for their formation.	5. Microemulsions are obtained by gentle mixing of ingredients.
6. Most of the emulsions are opaque (white) in appearance.	6. Microemulsions are transparent or translucent in nature.

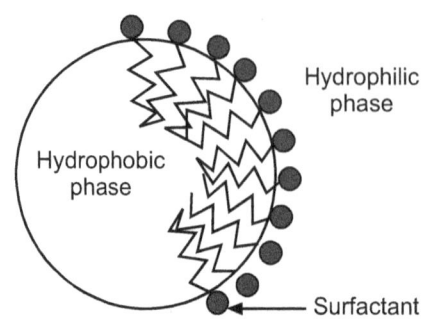

Surfactant: Forms the interfacial film

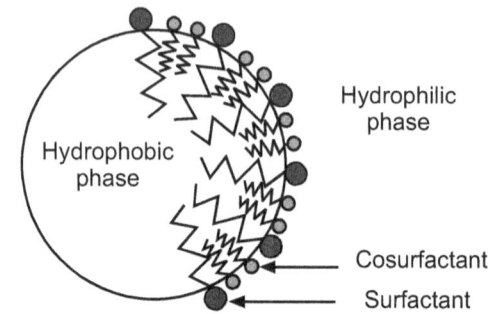

Surfactant: Forms the interfacial film

Co Surfactant: Ensures flexibility of
interfacial layer which
reduces the interfacial
tension

(a) Emulsion   **(b) Microemulsion**

Fig. 3.21: Basic difference between emulsion and microemulsion

Ingredients of Microemulsion:

Various ingredients are used in the formulation and development of microemulsions. Mainly oil and surfactants are used in microemulsion. They should be biocompatible, non-toxic and clinically acceptable. Main components of microemulsion are:

1. Oil phase
2. Aqueous phase
3. Surfactant
4. Cosurfactant

3.15.1 Methods of Formulation

- Microemulsions are prepared when interfacial tension at the oil/water is kept at very low level. Interfacial layer is kept very much flexible and fluid concentration of surfactants should be high enough to give surfactant molecules to be stabilized the microemulsion at an extremely low interfacial tension.

- **Two main methods reported for the formulation of microemulsion are :**
    1. Phase Inversion Method
    2. Phase Titration Method

1. Phase Inversion Method:

- In the phase inversion method phase inversion of microemulsions occurs by addition of excess amount of the dispersed phase.

- During phase inversion, quick physical changes occur including changes in particle size that can affect drug release both *in vivo* and *in vitro*. For non-ionic surfactants, this can be completed by changing the temperature, forcing a transition from oil-in-water microemulsion at low temperatures to water-in-oil microemulsion at higher temperatures (transitional phase inversion).

- During cooling, the system crosses a point of zero spontaneous curvature and minimal surface tension, promoting the formation of finely dispersed oil droplets. This method is also known as phase inversion temperature (PIT) method.

- Other than temperature, parameters such as pH value or salt concentration may be considered more effectively instead of the temperature alone.

- Additionally, a transition in the spontaneous radius of curvature can be obtained by changing the water volume fraction. By successively adding water into oil, initially water droplets are formed in a continuous oil phase.

- By increasing the water volume fraction changes the spontaneous curvature of the surfactant from initially stabilizing a w/o microemulsion to an o/w microemulsion at the inversion point.

2. Phase Titration Method:

- Microemulsions are prepared by the spontaneous emulsification method (phase titration method) and can be depicted with the help of phase diagrams. Construction of phase diagram is a useful approach to study the complex series of interactions that can occur when different components are mixed. Microemulsions are formed along with various association structures (including emulsion, micelles, lamellar, hexagonal, cubic and various gels and oily dispersion) depending on the chemical composition and concentration of each component. The understanding of their phase equilibrium and demarcation of the phase boundaries are essential aspects of the study. As quaternary phase diagram (four component system) is time consuming and difficult to interpret, pseudo ternary phase diagram is often constructed to find the different zones including microemulsion zone, in which each corner of the diagram represents 100% of the particular component (Fig. 3.22). The region can be separated into w/o or o/w microemulsion by simply considering the composition that is whether it is oil rich or water rich. Observations should be made carefully so that the metastable systems are not included.

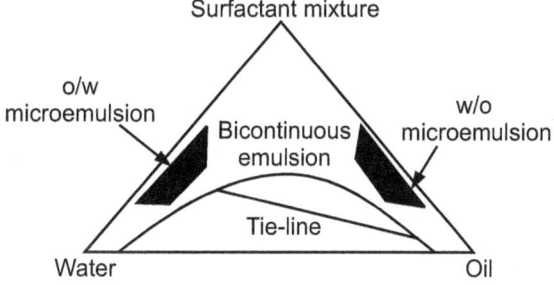

Fig 3.22: Pseudoternary phase diagram of oil, water and surfactant showing microemulsion region

3.15.2 Other Applications of Microemulsion

- Microemulsion in enhanced oil recovery.
- Microemulsions as fuels.
- Microemulsions as lubricants, cutting oils and corrosion inhibitors.
- Microemulsions as coatings and textile finishing.
- Microemulsions in detergency.
- Microemulsions in cosmetics.
- Microemulsions in agrochemicals.
- Microemulsions in food.
- Microemulsions in environmental remediation and detoxification.
- Microporous media synthesis (microemulsion gel technique).
- Microemulsions in analytical applications.
- Microemulsions as liquid membranes.

3.16 Evaluation of Emulsion

1. Tests Used to Identify Emulsion Type:

Since emulsion (o/w or w/o) looks the same in appearance with naked eyes, therefore certain tests have been developed to differentiate between them. At least two tests should be done to reach a conclusive decision about the identity of the emulsion.

(a) Dilution test: In this test, the emulsion is diluted either with oil or water. If the emulsion is o/w type and it is diluted with water, it will remain stable as water is the dispersion medium but if it is diluted with oil, the emulsion will break as oil and water are not miscible with each other. Oil-in-water emulsion can easily be diluted with an aqueous solvent whereas water-in-oil emulsion can be diluted with an oily liquid.

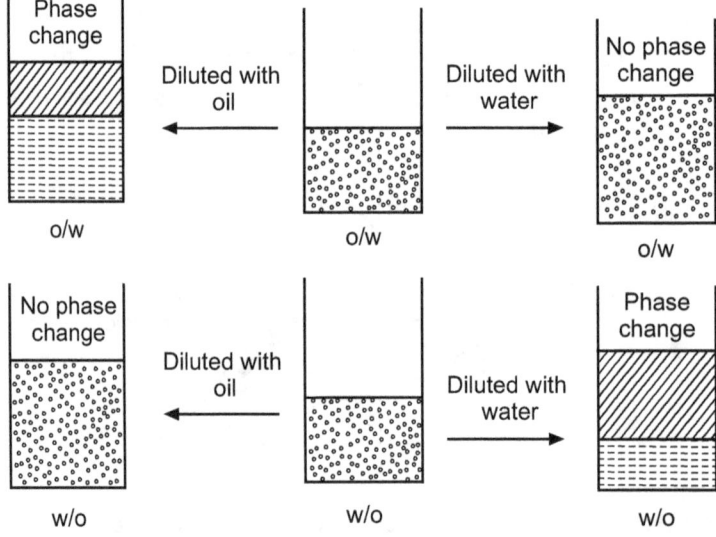

Fig. 3.23: Dilution test for o/w and w/o type emulsion

(b) Conductivity test: This test is based on the basic principle that water is a good conductor of electricity. Therefore in case of o/w emulsion, this test will be positive as water is the external phase. In this test, an assembly consisting of a pair of electrodes connected to a lamp is dipped into an emulsion. If the emulsion is o/w type, the lamp glows.

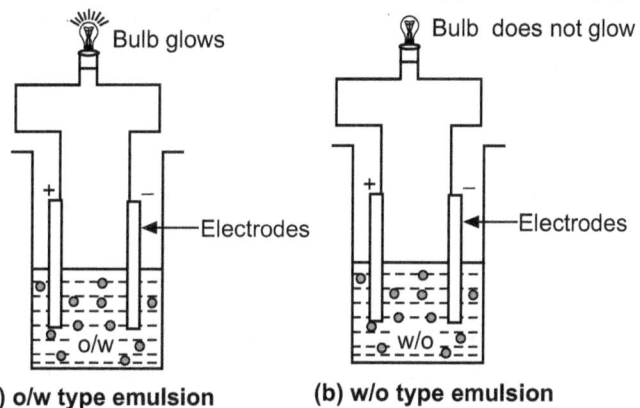

(a) o/w type emulsion   (b) w/o type emulsion

Fig. 3.24: Conductivity test for o/w and w/o type emulsion

(c) Dye solubility test: In this test, when an emulsion is mixed with a water soluble dye such as amaranth and observed under the microscope, if the continuous phase appears red, then it means that the emulsion is o/w type as water is the external phase and the dye will dissolve in it to give colour. But if the scattered globules appear red and continuous phase colourless, then it is w/o type. Similarly, if an oil soluble dye such as Scarlet red C or Sudan III is added to an emulsion and the continuous phase appears red, then it w/o emulsion.

(d) Cobalt chloride test: In this test, filter paper is soaked in cobalt chloride solution, dried and used for the test.

Dry cobalt chloride paper is blue in colour. When it comes in contact with water, the paper turns pink.

In order to determine the type of emulsion, the cobalt chloride paper is dipped in an emulsion. If the paper turns pink, it indicates presence of o/w type emulsion.

(e) Fluorescence test: If an emulsion on exposure to ultra-violet radiations shows continuous florescence under microscope, then it is w/o type and if it shows only spotty fluorescence, then it is o/w type.

2. **Globule Size:**
   - Growth in the globule size of emulsion is sign of physical instability.
   - Therefore size of globule and its distribution is generally ascertained in the emulsion over a certain period of time.
   - Initially, globule size may increase due to insufficient coverage by surfactant, but in good emulsion the globule gets stabilized after complete coverage, if globule size grows continuously then it is indicative of poor product.

- Globule size is measured by microscopic methods or by electronic devices such as coulter counter. In this technique, samples should be suitably diluted before estimation.
- Globule size also determines the appearance of emulsion and vice versa as below.

Table 3.5 : Appearance of emulsion according to globule size

Globule size (mm)	Appearance
> 1	White
0.1 - 1.0	Blue - White
0.05 - 0.1	Opalescent, Semitransparent
< 0.5	Transperant

3. **Viscosity:**
   - Viscosity determination is essential to access the stability of the emulsion. Viscosity is measured by using cone plate viscometers, penetrometers and brookfield viscometer.
   - Cone and plate viscometers are suitable for emulsions but instrument using co-axial cylinders are easy to use.
   - If the preparation is viscous, then penetrometers can be used.
   - Brookfield viscometers are useful in detection of creaming tendancy of emulsions, hence from rheological studies the long term behaviour of emulsion can be studied.
   - Capillary of falling sphere type of viscometer should be avoided.

4. **Electrophoretic Properties:**
   - Determination of electrophoretic properties like zeta potential is useful for assessing flocculation since electrical charges on particles influence the rate of flocculation.
   - O/W emulsion having a fine particle size will exhibit low resistance but if the particle size increases, then it indicates a sign of oil droplet aggregation and instability.

5. **Phase Separation:**
   - Phase separation is a phenomenon of changes in the emulsion type in which the emulsion may spontaneously revert from o/w to w/o and vice versa.
   - This may be estimated visually or by measuring the volume of separated phase.
   - It is checked by withdrawing a samples from top and bottom and comparing the composition of the two samples by appropriate analysis of water content, oil content or any suitable constituent.
   - Accelerating the separation by centrifugation followed by appropriate analysis of the specimen may be useful to quantitatively determine the phase separation.
   - High speed centrifugation (2,00,000 r.p.m.) can be used to test the strength of interfacial film.
   - At this, much speed emulsions with low strength interfacial film would crack up completely while the emulsions with tough interfacial films may survive.

6. **pH:**
   - pH is an important physical parameter and fluctuation in pH is not desirable as some drugs shows maximum stability at a specific pH value.
   - The measurement of the pH value provides good control over the manufacturing process and shelf life of the product.
   - The pH of emulsions is determined by using digital pH meter.
   - The values should be taken in triplicate and then average values are calculated.

7. **Redisperibility:**
   - The evaluation of redispersibility is also important. To quantitate this parameter to some extent, a mechanical shaking device may be used. It simulates human arm motion during the shaking process and can give reproducible result when used under controlled conditions.

3.17 Stress Testing

   - The final acceptance of an emulsion depends on stability, appearance and functionality of the packaged product.
   - There is no quick and sensitive method for determining potential instability in an emulsion to the formulator. So to speed up the stability test program the emulsion is subjected to various stress conditions. The stress testing is employed to evaluate the stability of emulsion.

The stress conditions normally employed include:

(i) Aging and Temperature, (ii) Centrifugation, and (iii) Agitation.

These stress conditions are described below :

(i) **Aging and Temperature:**
   - It is routine to determine the shelf life of all types of preparations by storing them for varying periods of time at temperatures that are higher than those normally encountered. The subjecting of emulsion at extremes and unrealistic temperature will give meaningless results. Many emulsions are stable at 40 to 45 °C but are unstable at 55 or 60 °C. So particularly for useful means of evaluating shelf life, a cycling should be conducted between two temperatures preferably between 4° and 45 °C.
   - The normal effect of aging an emulsion at elevated temperature is acceleration of the rate of coalescence or creaming, and this is usually coupled with changes in viscosity. Most emulsions become thinner at high temperature and thicken when cooled. Emulsion is affected by freezing than by warming. Crystals formed in formulation may exert pressure on the film and spherical shape of emulsion droplet may get affected.

(ii) **Centrifugation:**
   - Stoke's law shows that creaming is a function of gravity (g), and an increase in gravity therefore accelerates separation. Centrifugation at 3750 rpm in a 10 cm radius centrifuge for a period of 5 hours is equivalent to the effect of gravity for about one

year. Thus, shelf-life under normal storage conditions can be predicted rapidly by observing the separation of the dispersed phase due to either creaming or coalescence when the emulsion is exposed to centrifugation.

- The ultracentrifugation is another technique to study separation at extremely high speed approximately 25,000 r.p.m. Ultracentrifugation of emulsion shows three layers- uppermost layer of coagulated oil, an intermediate layer of uncoagulated emulsion and a pure aqueous layer. There will be rapid separation at 56,000 r.p.m. rate of separation is slower at 40,000 r.p.m. and there will be no separation at 11,000 r.p.m. This suggest that when adsorbed layer of emulsifier surrounding each droplet is broken, only then ultracentrifugation can cause separation of oil.

(iii) Agitation :

- Droplets in an emulsion exhibit Brownian movement. Due to this, droplets impinge upon each other and Coalescence takes place. Simple mechanical agitation contributes to the energy, with which two droplets impinge upon each other.
- Thus, agitation can also break emulsion. A typical example of coalescence by agitation is the manufacture of butter from milk.
- Conventional emulsions may deteriorate from gentle rocking on a reciprocating shaker. This works in two ways:
  (i) increases the rate of impingement of droplets, and
  (ii) reduction of viscosity of a normally thixotrophic system.

EXERCISE

1. What are emulsions and emulsifying agents? Give examples.
2. What are the theories of emulsification?
3. Explain the concept of HLB.
4. Write a note on Krafft point and Cloud point.
5. Write a note on stability of emulsions.
6. What is steric stabilization?
7. Explain in detail evaluation of emulsion.
8. Write note on antioxidants used in emulsion.
9. Explain creaming of an emulsion.
10. Explain how centrifugation and agitation can be used to assess the stability of an emulsion.
11. Define microemulsion. What are the advantages and disadvantages of microemulsion?
12. What is phase inversion temperature?
13. Write a note on Microemulsion.
14. Discuss in short how a microemulsion can be evaluated.
15. Explain in detail Multiple emulsion.

✍ ✍ ✍

Chapter ... 4

Semisolid Dosage Forms

Contents...

4.1 Introduction

Semisolids are meant for external application to the broken and unbroken skin or to mucous membrane. They have been variously designated as ointments, creams, pastes, jellies, salves etc. Suppositories may be included in this category as they are the unit dosage forms.

For the successful formulation, the understanding of skin physiology and absorption mechanism is essential. Stratum corneum is major route for topical drugs but hair follicle, associated sebaceous glands and sweat glands also offers route for drug penetration.

4.2 Skin-Anatomy and Physiology

Skin basically has three regions i.e. uppermost epidermis, middle dermis and lower subcutaneous tissues.

(A) Epidermis:

Epidermis is the outermost layer of skin. It is composed of stratified squamous epithelial cells. These epithelial cells are held together by highly convulated interlocking bridges and are responsible for the unique integrity of the skin. Epidermis is thickest in the area of palms and soles. It consist of five layers,

1. **Stratum Corneum:** It is horny layer of dead and compacted keratinised cells with a density of 1.55. It is a uppermost layer of skin. It consists of acutely flattened, stacked and hexagonal cells. Stratum Corneum is a layer of metabolically inactive tissues. Layers of Stratum Corneum are formed and continuously replenished by the slow upward movement of cells which are produced by the basal cell layer of Stratum Germinativum. It is replenished about every two weeks in a mature adult.

2. **Stratum Lucidum:** It is below Stratum Corneum and above Stratum Granulosum. It is in the palm of hand and soles of the feet. It is a thin translucent and lucid layer.

3. **Stratum Granulosum:** It is a third layer, the cells of which appear to have granules in it, that stains to yield a mottled appearance.

4. **Stratum Spinosum:** It is a multicellular spinous layer in which the cells exhibit sharp suface protuberances.

5. **Stratum Germinativum:** Stratum Germinativum is the regenerative layer of the epidermis. It is a single layer of cubical or columnar cells. This layer has high mitotic index and constantly renews the epidermis.

In the thicker parts of the skin, the transition from the living cells of the germinativum zone to the dead, cornified cells of the stratum corneum is made through three layers i.e. Stratum Spinosum, Stratum Granulosum, Stratum Lucidum. Means living cells passes thorough these three layers to Stratum Corneum from Stratum Germinativum.

(B) Dermis:

It lies between epidermis and subcutaneous fatty region/subcutaneous tissue. It is a network of structural protein fibre i.e. collagen, reticulum and elastin which are embedded in semigel matrix of mucopolysacchride. This gel structure or network offers elasticity to the skin. Below the dermis, fibrous tissue open out and merge with the fat containing subcutaneous tissues.

The dermis requires a high blood supply to, convey nutrients, remove waste product, regulate pressure and temperature, mobilize defence force and contribute to the skin colour.

(C) Subcutaneous Tissues:

This layer consists of sheet of fat rich aerolar tissue. Large arteries and veins are present only in the superficial region.

(D) Skin Appendages:

The skin is interspersed with hair follicle and associated sebaceous gland, and with two types of sweat glands, eccrine and apocrine. Collectively these are referred to as skin appendages.

1. **Eccrine sweat glands:** Its function is to aid the heat control, it produces sweat and may also secrets drugs, proteins, antibodies and antigen.

2. **Apocrine sweat glands:** It secrets oily or milky secretions may be coloured, and contains proteins, lipids, lipoproteins and saccharides.

3. **Hair follicle:** It develops all over the skin, except lips, palms and soles.

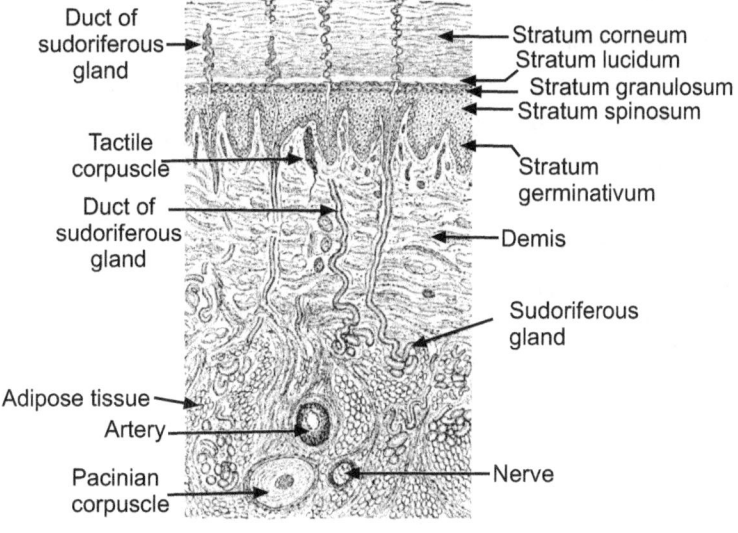

Fig. 4.1: Structure of skin

4.3 Percutaneous Absorption

The skin is made up of several layers including stratum corneum, viable epidermis and dermis, and it contains appendages that include sweat glands, sebaceous glands, and hair follicles.

The stratum corneum is the outermost 'horny' layer of skin, comprising about 15-20 rows of flat, partially desiccated, dead, keratinized epidermal cells.

The thickness of stratum corneum ranges from 10-20 μm, depending upon the region of the body, i.e. with the thickest layer on the palms of the hands and soles of the feet.

Of the various skin layers, stratum corneum is the rate-limiting barrier to percutaneous drug transport.

This layer is composed of about 40% lipids, 40% protein and only 20% water. So the transport of hydrophilic or charged molecules is especially difficult through the lipid-rich nature of the stratum corneum.

Transport of lipophilic drug molecules is facilitated by their dissolution into intercellular lipids around the cells of the stratum corneum. Similarly the absorption of hydrophilic molecules into skin can occur through 'pores' or openings of the hair follicles and sebaceous glands, but the relative surface area offered by these openings is barely 1% of the total skin surface.

This small surface area limits the amount of drug absorption.

Percutaneous absorption of drug molecules is of particular importance because the drug has to be absorbed to an adequate extent and rate, to achieve and maintain uniform, systemic, therapeutic levels throughout the duration of use.

In general, once drug molecules cross the stratum corneal barrier, its passage into deeper dermal layers and systemic uptake occurs relatively quickly and easily.

Generally, drug absorption into the skin occurs by passive diffusion. The rate of drug transport across the stratum corneum follows Fick's Law of Diffusion.

The rate of drug transport depends not only on its aqueous solubility, but is also directly proportional to its oil/water partition coefficient, its concentration in the formulation vehicle, and the surface area of the skin to which it is exposed; whereas the drug transport is inversely proportional to the thickness of the stratum corneum.

Fick's Law of Diffusion as applied to drug transport across stratum corneum :

$$\frac{dM}{dt} = \frac{D \cdot \Delta C \cdot K}{h}$$

where, $\frac{dM}{dt}$ is the steady-state flux across stratum corneum.

D is the diffusion coefficient or diffusivity of drug molecules.

ΔC is the drug concentration gradient across the stratum corneum.

K is the partition coefficient of the drug between skin and formulation medium, and

h is the thickness of the stratum corneum.

Importantly, for designing an effective topical or transdermal product, an understanding of the transport behaviour of drugs is vital.

So there are are two main routes of drug absorption/transport :

(i) The Transepidermal route and (ii) The Transfollicular route.

When a formulation is applied, then drug has to diffuse out passively from the vehicle in which it is formulated. Now, drug can partitioned into either the stratum corneum or sebum filled ducts of pilocebaceous glands, this depends on where the molecule is placed down.

Then drug moves down and reaches to viable epidermis and dermal points of entry, and by this way concentration gradient is established across the skin. The drug is swept away by the capillary flow and rapidly distributed throughout the body.

4.3.1 Percutaneous Absorption by the Transepidermal Route

The Transepidermal Route is the principal portal of entry because it offers large surface area 100 to 1000 times greater than other routes. By this route, diffusion occurs directly across the stratum corneum. Once a substance passes through the stratum corneum, there is no other obstacle to penetration of the remaining epidermal layers. There is then ready entry into the circulation via capillaries. The concentration gradient helps in reaching drug into circulation. The systemic circulation acts as a reservoir or *sinks for the drug*. In circulation, the drug is then diluted and distributed rapidly.

Transport of drug through Transepidermal Route involves following steps:

1. Dissolution of drug in vehicle.
2. Diffusion of drug from vehicle on skin.
3. Entering of drug into Trandepidermal route.
4. Partitioning of drug into stratum corneum.
5. Diffusion of drug through protein-lipid matrix of the stratum corneum.
6. Partitioning of drug into viable epidermis.
7. Diffusion of drug through cellular mass of epidermis.
8. Diffusion of drug through fibrous mass of upper dermis.
9. Capillary uptake of drug and entry of drug into systemic circulation.

4.3.2 Percutaneous Absorption by the Transfollicular/
Transappendageal Route

The appendages i.e. hair follicle and sweat glands offers relatively small surface area by this route, diffusion occurs through follicular route.

Transport of drug through Transfollicular Route involves following steps:

1. Dissolution of drug in vehicle.
2. Diffusion of drug from vehicle on skin.

3. Entering of drug into Transfollicular route.
4. Partitioning of drug into sebum.
5. Diffusion of drug through lipid in sebaceous pore/ecrine gland.
6. Partitioning of drug into viable epidermis.
7. Diffusion of drug through cellular mass of epidermis.
8. Diffusion of drug through fibrous mass of upper dermis.
9. Capillary uptake of drug and entry of drug into systemic circulation.

4.3.3 Flux and its Measurement

The drug diffusion through the skin is passive kinetic process that takes place down the concentration gradient from a region of high concentration to a region of lower concentration.

Flux is the amount of drug or permeant crossing the membrane per time.

The unit of flux is quantity/cm^2/min

It is calculated by following formula,

$$J = \frac{Q}{A} \times t$$

Where, J – Flux,

Q – Quantity of drug crossing the membrane in time t

A – Area available

4.3.4 Factors Affecting Percutaneous Absorption

Following factors affects the percutaneous absorption:

(I) Drug Related Factors:

1. **Drug concentration:** It is an important factor. The amount of drug percutaneously absorbed per unit surface area per time interval increases with increase in concentration.

2. **Particle size and Area of application:** More drug absorption depends on area of application. If area of application is larger then absorption will be more. Small particle size of drug allows easy and uniform application of formulation over larger surface.

3. **Physicochemical attraction to the skin:** The drug should have greater Physicochemical Attraction to the skin than vehicle. Because only then drug will come out of the vehicle and will be ready for absorption.

4. **Molecular weight:** Solutes with molecular weight below 400 dalton can penetrate the skin easily. Molecular weight is inversely proportional to the drug absorption, as small molecules penetrate faster than larger ones.

5. **Solubility:** The solute/drug should have both aqueous as well as lipid solubility for effective percutaneous absorption. Highly lipid soluble molecules enter through hair follicles. Moderately lipid soluble molecules penetrate directly across the horny layer.

6. **Partition coefficient:** It is important in determining the flux of drug through the membrane. Membrane is the source of diffusional resistance and diffusion of drug through stratum corneum usually provides rate limiting step in absorption. Hence, stratum corneum to vehicle partition coefficient of drug is delicatetly important in establishing a high initial concentration of diffusant in the first layer of the membrane. The drug with optimal log k, partition coefficient is required for good action.

7. **Melting point:** Drug should have low melting point for better absorption.

8. **Dose:** The potent drug with dose of 10-15 mg/day is desired.

9. **Crystal structure:** The metastable polymorph is much more soluble than its stable form, so the release of drug in metastable state is much faster than stable form.

(II) Patient Related Factors:

1. **Skin age:** It is one of the prime factor affecting drug permeation through the skin. Young skin is more permeable than older. The permeability of the skin is affected by age, disease, climate and injury.

2. **Blood supply:** Peripheral circulation affects transdermal permeation. Increased blood flow increases the flow of drug from dermis to systemic circulation.

3. **Thickness and nature of skin:** Thickness and nature of stratum corneum and density of appendages varies from person to person and it is responsible for cutaneous permeability. Percutaneous absorption appears to be greater when the drug is applied to the skin with a thin horney layer than with one that is thick. The horny layer is thickest on palms and soles and thinnest on the face; penetration rate increases with decreased thickness of horny layer.

4. **Species differences:** Skin thickness, density of appendages, keratinizaton, similarly sweating ability and blood supply affects penetration and resistance to permeation. In studies, it was observed that the monkey and pig skins are almost like that of humans.

5. **Hydration:** Hydration softens tissues, increases the size of the pore and allows the flow and increase the rate of passage of drugs through the skin. Hence, hydration of the skin is most important parameter in percutaneous absorption.

6. **Temperature:** Temperature changes on or in the skin are always accompanied by other physiological reactions, such as increased blood flow, or increased moisture content of the horny layer. These factors themselves can contribute to higher percutaneous absorption. Furthermore, increase in temperature increases drug solubility in both vehicle and stratum corneum and increases diffusivity, both of which will lead to a further increase in percutaneous absorption.

(III) Vehicle Related Factors:

The rate of release of a drug from a vehicle to stratum corneum is governed by *vehicle-to-stratum corneum partition coefficient*. The thermodynamic activity of the drug in the vehicle is the product of the concentration of the drug and the activity coefficient (γ) of the drug in the vehicle. Drugs held firmly by the vehicle exhibit low activity coefficient, hence slow rate of release from that drug-vehicle combination. Drug held loosely by the vehicle shows higher activity coefficient, hence shows faster rate of release.

The vehicles may enhance the penetration of a drug in one or more of the following ways:

(a) By ensuring good contact with the surface of the body.

(b) By increasing the degree of hydration of the stratum corneum.

(c) By penetrating the epidermis.

(d) By directly altering the permeability of the skin.

Following Vehicle Related Factors Affects Percutaneous Absorption:

1. **Miscibility:** Vehicles those readily mix with sebum and sweat and easily cover the skin surface can easily bring the drug into contact with the tissue cells and in such instances drug absorption is appeared to be enhanced.

2. **Hydration:** Vehicle must be capable of increasing moisture in the skin to help in percutaneous absorption. Vehicles effects on skin hydration, occlusive vehicles such as fats and oils reduce water loss and increase the moisture content and thus increases the drug penetration.

3. **Penetration:** Sovents such as water, alcohols and acetone play the dual role of Vehicle as well as Penetration enhancers.

4. **Drug-Vehicle affinity:** Vehicles should have low affinity for the penetrant for the penetration to occur, hence the selection of vehicles affects the release of substance from the system applied.

   When vehicle firmly holds solute it exhibit low activity coefficient hence the rate of release from such drug-vehicle combination is slow.

   When vehicle loosely holds solute, it exhibit high activity coefficient and the rate of release from such a drug-vehicle combination is fast.

5. **Effect on skin:** Vehicles should be non-irritant, non-toxic, and it must give emollient effect to skin making skin soft and smooth, similarly it should be easy to remove from skin and clothings.

6. **Contact with body surface:** Sticky bases such as oleaginous bases adheres well to the skin but are difficult to apply evenly and remove completely.

   Creams are easier to apply and remove. Oil in water (o/w) creams mix with sebum and is more suitable for weeping or wounded surface.

7. **Alteration of skin permeability**: Penetration can be improved by dissolving the medicament in an organic liquid such as ethanol, dimethylformamide (DMF), dimethyl acetamide, dimethylsulfoxide (DMSO) and propylene glycol. They increase the hydration of skin and improves permeability.

4.4 Penetration Enhancers

This term has been used to describe substances that facilitate absorption through the skin. Transdermal drug delivery system is convenient route for the delivery of drugs having short biological half life. It is based on absorption of drugs through the skin after topical application. Penetration enhancers are the substances used to increase permeation of skin mucosa. Penetration enhancer increases the absorption of penetrant through the skin which is also known as 'absorption promoter' or 'absorption enhancers' or 'accelerants' which act by penetrating the skin and interfering with the barrier properties of the stratum cornium.

Various types of Penetration Enhancers are available, but most drugs penetrate better through the hydrated stratum corneum than through the dry tissue, hence Water is the best penetration enhancer as far as cost, safety and effectiveness is concerned.

4.4.1 Ideal Properties of Penetration Enhancers

1. It should be non-toxic, non-irritating, pharmacologically inert, non-allergic.
2. It should be compatible with drug and excipients and skin.
3. It should be odourless, colourless, tasteless and inexpensive and should have good solvent properties.
4. It should not give pharmacological activity within body.
5. It should be cosmetically acceptable.
6. It should be chemically and physically stable.
7. Its duration of action should be both predictable and reproducible.
8. It should work rapidly.
9. It should be tested in research laboratories.

4.4.2 Advantages of Penetration Enhancers

1. It increases the delivery of ionisable drugs. Example: timolol maleate etc.
2. It is used to maintain the level of drug concentration in blood.
3. It improves the efficacy of less potent drugs with higher dose. Example: oxymorphane.
4. It is used to deliver the impermeable drugs. Example: heparin etc.
5. It is used to deliver the drugs having high molecular weight like peptide and hormones.

4.4.3 Disadvantages of Penetration Enhancers

1. The uses of different penetration enhancer with various concentrations are restricted completely.
2. **Penetration Enhancers** may show side effects in the body.
3. The effectivenss of **Penetration Enhancers will vary from drug to drug**.

4.4.4 Types of Penetration Enhancers

Table 4.1 : Types of penetration enhancers and their mechanism

Types/Techniques	Mechanism of action	Examples
1. Chemical enhancers	They act by three mechanisms 1. By disrupting the highly ordered structure of stratum corneum lipid. 2. By interacting with intercellular protein. 3. By enhancing the partition of the drug or solvent into stratum corneum.	1. Sulphoxides and similar chemicals- dimethyl sulphoxide (DMSO), dimethyl formamide (DMF), dimethyl acetamide (DMAC) 2. Azones 3. Pyrrolidones 4. Fatty acids - Lauric acid, Myristic acid and capric acid 5. Oxizolidinones (4-decycloxazolidine-2-one) 6. Amine and Amides - Urea 7. Surface active agents - sodium lauryl sulphate, Benzalkonium chloride 8. Cyclodextrins
2. Drug Vehicle Based	Interaction of enhancers with stratum corneum and development of SAR for enhances with optimal characteristics and minimal toxicity.	Ion pairs and complex coacervates chemical potential adjustment.
3. Natural Penetration Enhancers	Mechanism for Terpenes It may increase one or more of following effects. 1. Partition coefficient 2. Diffusion coefficient 3. Lipid extraction 4. Drug solubility 5. Macroscopic barrier perturbation 6 Molecular orientation of terpenes molecule with lipid bilayer	1. Terpens - Menthol, Linalool, Limonene, Carvacrol. 2. Essential oil - Basil oil, Neem oil, Eucalyptus, Chenopodium, Ylang-Ylang.
4. Physical Enhancers	These are variable techniques available for increasing the penetration by physical separation and magnetic and ultrasonic	1. Iontophoresis 2. Sonophoresis 3. Phonophoresis 4. Magnetophoresis 5. Electroporation 6. Thermophoresis 7. Radiofrequency 8. Hydration of stratum corneum 9. Stripping of stratum corneum

... (Contd.)

Types/Techniques	Mechanism of action	Examples
5. Biochemical Approach	They act by modifying substances by converting it into suitable form.	1. Synthesis of bio-convertible pro drugs. 2. Co-administration of skin metabolite inhibitors.
6. Miscellaneous Enhancers	Having various mechanism	1. Lipid synthesis inhibitors 2. Phospholipids 3. Clofibric acid 4. Dodecyl - N, N-Dimethyl

4.4.5 Functions of Penetration Enhancers

Penetration Enhancers majorly performs following functions on the basis of lipid protein partitioning concept.

1. **Protein modification:** Certain Penetration Enhancers such as Surfactants, and DMSO interact with protein *Keratin* and opens dense structure of stratum corneum and increases the permeability.

2. **Lipid disruption:** Many agents like azones terpenes, fatty acids , alcohols and DMSO interact with organised intercellular lipid structure of stratum corneum so as to disrupt it and thereby increase the permeability.

3. **Partitioning promotion:** Solvents like ethanol enter the stratum corneum and changes its solvent properties and thus increases the partitioning of second molecule in the horny layer. This molecule may be a drug, co-enhancer or a co-solvent.

4.5 Selection Criterion for Bases

A number of ointment bases are available but no single base satisfies all the requirements of formulation. Bases are selected by considering the pharmaceutical and dermatological factors. When single base is not enough then combination of one or more bases is preferred.

1. Dermatological factors
2. Pharmaceutical factors

1. Dermatological Factors:

(a) Absorption and penetration: Absorption and Penetration are two different terms as far as the semisolids are concerned.

'Penetration' means passage of the drug across the skin i.e. cutaneous penetration, and 'Absorption' means passage (entry) of the drug into blood stream.

Following are the some results of experiment:

• Bases penetrates the skin and medicament absorbed through the skin.

• Medicaments which are both soluble in oil and water are most readily absorbed though the skin.

• Water soluble substances can be readily absorbed from water soluble bases.

- Paraffins do not penetrate the skin.
- Whereas animal and vegetable fats and oils normally penetrate the skin.
- Animals fats, e.g. lard and wool fat when combined with water, penetrates the skin.
- o/w emulsion bases release the medicament more readily than greasy bases or w/o emulsion bases.

(b) Effect on the skin:

- Bases should not interfere with the function of skin that may lead to discomfort to the person.
- Greasy bases mainly interfere with normal skin functions such as heat radiation and sweating. They are irritant to the skin.
- The greasy bases forms occlusive film over skin and sweat remains below the film and due to which sweat does not come out and person may feel heating sensation.
- The less greasy bases such as o/w emulsion bases and other water miscible bases produce a cooling effect due to the removal of sweat and evaporation of water.
- These bases mix readily with the skin.

(c) **Miscibility with skin secretion and sebum:** Base should be miscible with the skin secretions and sebum because only then the drug will completely and rapidly release to the skin hence lesser proportion of the medicament is required when such miscible bases are used. Skin secretions are more readily miscible with the emulsion bases than with greasy bases.

(d) **Compatibility with skin secretions:** The bases used should be compatible with skin secretions. The average skin secretions have pH about 5.5, so the bases with pH around 5.5 are used to get compatibility. Generally, neutral ointment bases are preferred.

(e) **Non-irritant:** All bases should be highly pure and bases especially for eye ointments should be non-irritant and free from foreign particles.

(f) **Emollient properties:** The bases should have emollient properties. Dryness and brittleness of the skin causes discomfort to the skin therefore, the bases should keep the skin moist. For this purpose, water and humectants such as glycerin, propylene glycol are used. Ointments should prevent rapid loss of moisture from the skin. Ointments having woolfat and liquid paraffin also act as emollient because they prevent rapid loss of water from the skin.

(g) **Ease of application and removal:** The ointment bases should be easily applicable as well as easily removable from the skin and clothings by simple washing with water. Stiff and sticky ointment bases require much force to spread on the skin and during rubbing newly formed tissues on the skin may be damaged. Hence, emulsion bases are preferred as they are softer and spread more easily and uniformly over the area of application. Emulsion bases are easy to remove from skin and clothing simply by washing with water.

2. Pharmaceutical Factors:

(a) Stability: Stability is an important parameter for formulation, so bases used in semisolids should be stable to give acceptable formulation. Fats and oils obtained from animal and plant sources are prone to oxidation unless they are suitably preserved. Due to oxidation, odour comes out. This type of reactions are called *rancidification*. Lard, from animal origin, rancidify rapidly. Soft paraffin, simple ointment and paraffin ointment are inert and stable. Liquid paraffin and its ointment is also stable but after prolonged storage it gets oxidized. O/W type emulsion bases are liable to microbial growth and needs a proper preservation. This can be prevented by incorporating a suitable antioxidant in desired concentration. Therefore, an antioxidant like *tocopherol* (Vit-E) may be incorporated. Other antioxidants those may be used are *butylated hydroxy toluene* (BHT) or *butylated hydroxy anisole* (BHA).

(b) Solvent properties: The base should have good solvent properties. Most of the medicaments used in the preparation of ointments are insoluble in the ointment bases therefore; they are finely powdered and are distributed uniformly throughout the base. If single base is not sufficient then a mixture of bases is recommended.

(c) Emulsifying properties: Hydrocarbon bases absorbs very small amount of water.

Animal fats absorb a large quantity of water.

Wool fat can take about 50% of water and when mixed with other fats, can take up several times its own weight of aqueous solution.

Emulsifying ointment, cetrimide emulsifying ointment and cetomacrogol emulsifying ointment are capable of absorbing considerable amount of water, forming w/o creams.

(d) Consistency: The ointments produced should be of suitable consistency. They should neither be hard nor too soft. They should withstand climatic conditions. Thus, in summer they should not become too soft and in winter not too hard to be difficult to remove from the container and spread on the skin.

The consistency of an ointment base can be controlled by varying the ratio of hard paraffin when formulation is too soft and liquid paraffin when formulation is too hard.

4.6 Ointment Bases

The ointment base is that substance or part of an ointment preparation which serves as carrier or vehicle for the medicament.

An ideal ointment base should be inert, stable-physically and chemically, smooth - free from grittiness, compatible with the skin, non-irritating and should release the incorporated medicaments readily. There is no single base which satisfies all the above properties so, the combination is needed to fulfill formulation and patient requirements.

Selection of the Appropriate Base:

It depends on careful assessment of a number of factors such as:

- Desired release rate of the drug substance from the ointment base.

- Desirability of topical or percutaneous drug absorption.
- Desirability of occlusion of moisture from the skin.
- Stability of the drug in the ointment base.
- Effect of the drug on the consistency or other features of the ointment base.
- Desire for a base easily removed by washing with water.
- Characteristics of the surface to which it is applied.

4.6.1 Classification of Ointment Bases

1. Oleaginous bases
2. Absorption bases
3. Water-miscible bases
4. Water soluble bases

1. Oleaginous Bases/Hydrocarbon Bases:

These bases consists of oils and fats. Oleaginous bases are also termed as hydrocarbon bases. On application to the skin, they have an emollient effect and protect against the escape of moisture. They can remain on the skin for relatively long periods without drying, and because of their immiscibility with water are difficult to wash off. Water and aqueous preparations may be incorporated, but only in small amounts and with some difficulty. Petrolatum (Vaseline) is an example of hydrocarbon bases. When powdered substances are to be incorporated into hydrocarbon bases, liquid petrolatum (mineral oil) may be used as the levigating agent.

The most important are the *Hydrocarbons* i.e. petrolatum, paraffins and mineral oils. The combination of these materials can produce a product of desired melting point and viscosity.

(a) Petrolatum (Soft paraffin):

- This is a purified mixture of semi-solid hydrocarbons obtained from petroleum or heavy lubricating oil.

Yellow soft paraffin (Petrolatum; Petroleum jelly)

- This is a purified mixture of semisolid hydrocarbons obtained from petroleum.
- It is yellow coloured odourless viscous base.
- It may contain suitable stabilizers like, antioxidants e.g. α-tocopherol (Vitamin E), butylated hydroxy toluene (BHT) etc.
- Melting range : 38 to 56°C.

White soft paraffin (White petroleum jelly, White petrolatum)

- This is a purified mixture of semisolid hydrocarbons obtained from petroleum.
- It is wholly or partially decolourized by percolating the yellow soft paraffin through freshly burned bone black or adsorptive clays or by bleaching.
- **Use:** The white form is used when the medicament is colourless, white or a pastel shade.

- Melting range: 38 to 56°C.
- It is not used in the ophthalmic preparations because traces of bleaching agent if present may harm the eye.

(b) Hard paraffin (Paraffin):
- This is a mixture of solid hydrocarbons obtained from petroleum.
- It is colourless or white, odourless, translucent, wax-like substance.
- It solidifies between 50 and 57°C and is used to stiffen ointment bases.

(c) Liquid paraffin (Liquid petrolatum; White mineral oil):
- It is a mixture of liquid hydrocarbons obtained from petroleum by distillation.
- It is transparent, colourless, odourless, tasteless, viscous liquid.
- On long storage, it may oxidize to produce peroxides and therefore, it may contain tocopherol or BHT as antioxidants.
- It is used along with hard paraffin and soft paraffin to get a desired consistency of the ointment.
- Tubes for eye, rectal and nasal ointments have nozzles with narrow orifices through which it is difficult to expel very viscous ointments without the risk of bursting the tube. To facilitate the extrusion, upto 25% of the base may be replaced by liquid paraffins.

Advantages of Hydrocarbons Bases:
1. They are not absorbed by the skin and remain on the skin surface as an occlusive layer which restricts the loss of moisture hence, keeps the skin soft.
2. They ensure prolonged contact between skin and medicament because of sticky nature.
3. They are almost inert.
4. They consist largely of saturated hydrocarbons; therefore, very few incompatibilities and little tendency of rancidity are there.
5. They can withstand heat sterilization; hence, sterile ophthalmic ointments can be prepared with it.
6. They are readily available and cheap.

Disadvantages of Hydrocarbon Bases:
1. They prevent drainage on oozing areas and also prevent evaporation of cutaneous secretions along with perspiration.
2. It retains body heat, which may produce a discomfort and feeling of warmth.
3. They are immiscible with water; as a result application and removal after treatment both are difficult.
4. They are sticky and do not help in absorption of medicaments.
5. Water absorption capacity of these bases is very low.

2. Absorption Bases:

The term 'absorption base' is used to denote the water absorbing or emulsifying property of these bases and not to describe their action on the skin.

These bases (some times called *emulsifiable ointment bases*) are generally anhydrous substances which have property of absorbing (emulsifying) considerable amount of water but still retaining their ointment like consistency.

Preparations of this type do not contain water as a component of their basic formula but if water is incorporated a w/o emulsion results.

(a) Wool fat (Anhydrous lanolin):

- It is the purified anhydrous fat like substance obtained from the wool of sheep.
- It is also known as anhydrous Lanolin.
- It is practically insoluble in water but can absorb water upto 50% of its own weight. Due to its sticky nature it is not used alone but is used along with other bases in the preparation of a number of ointments.
- It is used in simple ointments base and eye ointment base.
- Example: Simple ointment B.P. contains 5% and the B.P. eye ointment base contains 10% woolfat.

(b) Hydrous wool fat (Lanolin):

- It is a mixture of 70 % w/w wool fat and 30 % w/w purified water. It is a w/o emulsion. Aqueous liquids can be emulsified with it.
- It is insoluble in water but soluble in ether and chloroform.
- It is used alone as an emollient.
- **Example:** Hydrous Wool Fat Ointment B.P.C., Calamine Coal Tar Ointment.

(c) Wool alcohol:

- It is the emulsifying fraction of wool fat.
- Wool alcohol is obtained from wool fat by treating it with alkali and separating the fraction containing cholesterol and other alcohols. It contains not less than 30% of cholesterol.
- It is used as an emulsifying agent for the preparation of w/o emulsions and is used to absorb water in ointment bases.
- It is also used to improve the texture, stability and emollient properties of o/w emulsions.
- **Examples:** Wool alcohol ointment B.P. contains 6% wool alcohol and hard, liquid and soft paraffin.

(d) Beeswax:

- It is purified wax, obtained from honey comb of bees.
- It contains small amount of cholesterol. It is of two types: (a) yellow beeswax and (b) white beeswax. White bees wax is obtained by bleaching yellow bees wax.
- Beeswax is used as a stiffening agent in ointment preparations.
- **Examples:** Paraffin ointment B.P.C. contains beeswax.

(c) Cholesterol:

- It is widely distributed in animal organisms. Wool fat is also used as a source of cholesterol.
- It is used to increase the water absorbing power of an ointment base.
- **Example:** Hydrophilic petroleum U.S.P.

Advantages of Absorption Bases:

1. These are less occlusive nevertheless, are good emollient.
2. These are easier to spread.
3. They assists oil soluble medicaments to penetrate the skin.
4. They are compatible with majority of the medicaments.
5. They are relatively heat stable.
6. The base may be used in their anhydrous form or in emulsified form.
7. They can absorb a large quantity of water or aqueous substances.

Disadvantage of Absorption Bases:

1. Inspite of their hydrophilic nature, absorption bases are difficult to wash and somewhat greasy.

3. Emulsion Bases:

- They are miscible with an excess of water.
- Ointments made from Emulsion bases are easily removed after use.
- There are two types of emulsion bases o/w and w/o emulsion bases.
- o/w emulsion bases are more popular because they can be easily removed from the skin and clothing.
- o/w bases are less or not greasy because water is in external phase and W/O bases are greasy and sticky as oil is in external phase.

Advantages of Emulsion Bases:

1. It is readily miscible with the exudates from lesions.
2. It reduces interference with normal skin function.
3. It enhances Good contact with the skin, because of their surfactant content.
4. It has high cosmetic acceptability.
5. It can be easily removed from the skin.

4. **Water Soluble Bases:**
   - Water soluble bases contain only the water soluble ingredients and not the fats or other greasy substances, hence, they are known as grease-less bases.
   - Water soluble bases consists of water soluble ingredients such as polyethylene glycol polymers (PEG) which are popularly known as "carbowaxes" and commercially known as "macrogols".
   - The carbowaxes are water soluble non-volatile, inert ingradients.
   - Depending upon the molecular weight, carbowaxes are available in different consistancies i.e. liquid, semisolids and solids.
   - Their molecular weight varies from 200 to 8000.
   - Different PEGs are mixed to get an ointment of desired consistency.
   - Certain other substances which are used as water soluble ointment bases include tragacanth, gelatin, pectin, silica gel, sodium alginate, cellulose derivatives etc.

   Example:

Macrogols 200, 300, 400	– viscous liquids
Macrogols 1500	– greasy semi-solids
Macrogols 1540, 3000, 4000, 6000	– waxy solids.

Advantages of PEGs as Ointment Base:
1. They are water soluble non-greasy; hence, can be removed easily from the skin and readily miscible with tissue exudates.
2. It has compatibility with skin and many dermatological medicaments.
3. It helps in good absorption by the skin.
4. It has good solvent properties. Some water-soluble dermatological drugs, such as salicylic acid, sulfonamides, sulfur etc. are soluble in this bases.
5. They do not hydrolyze, rancidify or support microbial growth.

Disadvantages of PEGs as Ointment Base:
1. Limited uptake of water.
2. Reduction in activity of certain antibacterial agents, e.g. phenols, hydroxybenzoates and quaternary compounds.

4.7 Ointments

Ointments are soft semisolid preparations meant for external application to the skin or mucous membrane.

They usually contains medicament which is either dissolved or suspended in the base.

They have emollient and protective action.

4.7.1 Classification of Ointments

According to their therapeutic properties based on penetration of skin.

(a) Epidermic, (b) Endodermic, (c) Diadermic.

(a) **Epidermic ointments:** These ointments are intended to produce their action on the surface of the skin and produce local effect. They are not absorbed. They act as protectives, antiseptics and parasiticides.

(b) **Endodermic ointments:** These ointments are intended to release the medicaments that penetrate into the skin. They are partially absorbed and acts as emollients, stimulants and local irritants.

(c) **Diadermic ointments:** These ointments are intended to release the medicaments that pass through the skin and produce systemic effects.

4.7.2 Formulation of Ointments

Drug:

Drug can be formulated in semisolid dosage form for their local or systemic effect. Drug may be soluble or insoluble; it must be able to cross lipoidal stratum corneum and hydrophilic viable epidermis and dermis so as to get systemic effect.

Drug should have sufficient solubility in vehicle but it must not posses' higher affinity towards it, because if drug shows higher affinity, it will be difficult to pull out the drug from vehicle and making it insufficient for release, hence for certain instances suspended (insoluble) drug has better drug release than dissolved drug.

Vehicles:

There are various bases available, which can be used either single or in combination with the other to fulfil pharmaceutical and dermatological requirements.

Example:

(I) Oleaginous Bases:

Hydrocarbons: Petrolatum, Microcrystalline wax, Paraffin Wax, Plastibase (Jelene), Liquid paraffin, Ceresi.

Vegetable oils and Animal fat: Coconut oil, Bees wax, Olive oil, Lanolin, Peanut oil, Spermaceti wax, Sesame oil, Almond oil.

Hydrogenated and Sulphated oils: Hydrogenated castor, Cotton seed, Soyabeen corn oils, Hydrogenated sulphated caster oils.

Alcohols, Acids and Esters: Cetyl alcohol, Stearic acid, Stearyl alcohol, Oleic acid, Oleyl alcohol, Palmitic acid, Lauryl alcohol. Lauraic acid, Myristyl alcohol, Ethyl oleate, Isopropyl myristicate, Ethylene glycol.

Silicones: Dimethylpropylsiloxanes, Methyl phenyl polysiloxanes, Steryl esters of dimethyl polysiloxanes.

(II) Absorption Bases:

Wool alcohol lanoline, bees wax, cholesterol, woolfat

(III) Emulsion Bases:

o/w emulsion base, w/o emulsion base

(IV) Water Soluble Bases:

Carbowaxes

Buffers:

The buffers are added to resist the change in pH, to maintain the stability, to enhance solubility and to improve the compatibility of the formulation. Skin has weak acidic nature hence tolerates weak acidic preparations than alkaline preparations. Buffers like sodium acetate, sodium citrate are used.

Preservatives:

The oil based preparations do not provide good media for microbial growth; but ointments having water require protection against microbial contamination. Microbial contamination affects potency and stability of the product.

Before the addition of the preservatives their quantities should be carefully decided. While selection of preservatives the parameters like irritancy or toxicity of the compound to the tissue to which the ointment is to be applied should be taken into consideration. At the same time, the plastic containers or rubber closures may 'take up' some amount of the preservatives thus reducing their availability for antimicrobial action.

Sometimes the preservatives get complexed by other ingredients and are thus not available in sufficient concentration for preservation.

Example: Methyl and Propyl Paraben, Benzoic acid, Sodium benzoate, Phenol, Cresol, Benzolkonium Chloride etc.

Microbial contamination can also be overcome by sterilization or bacterial filtration.

Antioxidents:

Antioxidants should be included whenever there is a possibility of oxidative degradation of the base. It may be more desirable to select two antioxidants instead of one.

Antioxidants should be non-irritant, non-toxic, stable and compatible.

Generally, compounds like butylated hydroxy anisole, propyl gallate, tocopherol, nor dihydroguaiaretic acid etc. are used in ointment bases.

Chelating Agents:

Whenever it is anticipated that traces of metallic ions are likely to catalyse oxidative degradations, hence the addition of only antioxidents is not sufficient to block the oxidative chain reaction. So small amounts of substances such as citric acid, edetic acid, maleic acid, phosphoric acid etc. may be added to chelate the metallic ions causing oxidation.

Humectant:

Change in atmospheric condition may affect the formulation. Humectant is a substance used to minimize the water loss from semisolid and prevent formulation from drying out even if change in weather. Humactants like glycerol, propylene glycol and sorbitol can be used in semisolids.

Perfumes and Colours:

Most ointments these days have a pleasant smell and colour imparted by incorporation of perfume and colours. The selection of a perfume blend is a very tricky business and every manufacturer would like to give a distinctive odourific quality to his product. The perfumes selected must be compatible with other ingredients. Essential oils from plant materials are used as perfumes.

The floral group blends such odours as lavender, jasmine, rose, lily and gardenia. The woody is group characterized by sandal wood, cedar wood.

The semisolids should be creamy white or of faint appealing colour. The colours like Eosin, Fluorescine etc. are used.

4.7.3 Manufacturing of Ointments

Ointments are prepared by two methods, depending on the nature of the ingredients:

1. Incorporation Method:

The active ingredient and the ointment base are mixed together until a uniform preparation is obtained. On a small scale, the pharmacist may mix the components using a mortar and pestle, or a slab and spatula. On large scale (up to 1500 kg), ointments are manufactured in stainless steel tank which has a built-in mixer.

- Before the incorporation of the active ingredients, insoluble substances should first be reduced to desirable particle size and passed through the sieve no 85. So the final product will not be gritty.
- Dissolve the drug in water or oil according to its solubility, then this mixture is added into the aqueous or oily base.
- Alcoholic solutions of small volume may be added easily to both oleaginous or emulsion bases.
- Chloroform and alcohol are not be used as a co-solvent because when it evaporates it results into crystallization. But use of glycerine and propylene glycol can minimize the crystallization.
- Liquid drugs are added to an ointment only after consideration of an ointment base's capacity to accept the volume required. For example, only very small amounts of an aqueous solution may be incorporated into an oleaginous ointment, because it can not accept water whereas absorption bases readily accept more amounts of aqueous solutions.
- When it is necessary to add an aqueous preparation to a *hydrophobic* base (such as oleaginous base), in that case the solution first may be incorporated into a minimum amount of a *hydrophilic* base (such as absorption base) and then this mixture is added to the hydrophobic base. However, all bases, even if hydrophilic, have their limits to retain liquids, beyond which they become too soft or semiliquid.

- The small quantity of powder can be mixed with base by using spatula on ointment slab or it may be called spatulation. Spatula is useful in breaking the lumps if any. Again due to spatula, material transfer is also easy.
- White ointment slab is used for dark coloured ointment and vice-versa.

Example 1:

Whitfield ointment (Compound benzoic acid ointment BPC)

Formula:

Benzoic acid, in fine powder	6.0 gm
Salicylic acid, in fine powder	3.0 gm
Emulsifying ointment	91.0 gm

Procedure:

Benzoic acid is a fugistatic agent and Salicylic acid has keratolytic activity. Emulsifying agent is a base. This formulation is also called as Whitfields ointment and it is a antifungal preparation. This formulation is prepared by trituration method.

1. Sieve benzoic acid and salicylic acid through sieve no. 85.
2. Mix them on the tile with small amount of base and levigate until smooth and then add remaining quantities.
3. Mix properly and transfer the ointment to a suitable wide mouth air-tight container, label and dispense.
4. Label as - FOR EXTERNAL USE ONLY,

   DO NOT FREEZE,

   STORE IN COOL AND DRY PLACE,

   REPALCE CAP TIGHTLY AFTER USE,

   APPLY TO THE AFFECTED AREA.

Example 2: Sulphur ointment IP

Formula:

Sublimed sulphur	10.0 gm
Simple ointment, white	90.0 gm

Procedure:

Sulphur is used in the treatment of acne vulgaris, simple ointment is a base. Sublimed sulphur is obtained from sublimation of native sulphur, it is gritty powder, should be sifted finely before use.

1. Sift the sublimed sulphur through sieve no. 85.
2. Mix sulphur with small quantity of base, then gradually add remainder of the base.
3. Transfer ointment to a suitable wide mouth air-tight container, lable and dispense.

4. Label as - FOR EXTERNAL USE ONLY,

    DO NOT FREEZE,

    STORE IN COOL AND DRY PLACE,

    REPALCE CAP TIGHTLY AFTER USE,

    APPLY TO THE AFFECTED AREA.

2. Fusion Method:

In fusion method, all or some of the components of an ointment are melted together and cooled with constant stirring until congealed. Heat sensitive materials are not melted at the beginning (e.g. heat sensitive and volatile substances) are added last to the congealing mixture as it is being cooled and stirred. The bases having high melting point such as beeswax, paraffin, and high molecular weight PEGs, which cannot be mixed well by incorporation method, are prepared by fusion method.

Grate the waxy solids.

- First melt the ingredients with highest melting point.

- Then add other oil phase and solid ingredients into the mixture in decreasing order of their melting point. This will avoid over-heating of substances having low melting point.

- Avoid vigorous agitation to avoid entrapment of air into the formulation.

Example : Simple ointment B.P.

Formula:

Wool fat	5.0 gm
Hard paraffin	5.0 gm
Cetostearyl alcohol	5.0 gm
White soft paraffin	85.0 gm

Procedure:

1. Simple ointment B.P. is prepared by fusion method.

2. Melt hard paraffin and cetostearyl alcohol on water-bath. Then mix wool fat and white soft paraffin and stir until all the ingredients are melted.

3. Decant or strain if required, again stir the mixture thoroughly until cold and pack in suitable wide mouth container.

4. Label as - FOR EXTERNAL USE ONLY,

    DO NOT FREEZE,

    STORE IN COOL AND DRY PLACE,

    REPALCE CAP TIGHTLY AFTER USE.

4.8 Creams

Creams are semisolid emulsions and are generally of softer consistency and lighter than ointments. The creams are applied to the skin for protective, beautifying, therapeutic or prophylactic purpose. They are less greasy and are easy to apply. Basically, creams are emulsions. Creams consist of medicaments dissolved or suspended in water removable or emollient bases. Creams are classified as water/in oil or oil/in water therefore, combining immiscible compounds is possible by mechanical agitation or heat. Creams like o/w, contains water in its external phase hence can be removed easily from skin and clothing. Whereas w/o creams are somewhat difficult to remove. o/w creams promotes bacterial growth but w/o creams they do not.

Creams are topically applied to smooth and hydrate the skin, to cure the acne rash, bedsores and to protect from external sun radiations.

In the treatment, the vehicle may be as important as the active agent. Creams are appropriate for patients with sensitive or dry skin who require a non-irritating, non-drying formulation. So patient with dry skin will not complain of a "dry" feel with creams and may be more comfortable with creams, which have a oily effect. Topical application of the cream at the affected site helps in delivery of drug directly to the site of the action. Cream work best in patients with dry skin.

4.8.1 Classification of Creams

Creams are of following types-

1. According to type of emulsion base:

    (a) Oily Creams

    (b) Aqueous Cream

2. According to their function:

    (a) Cleansing Creams or Lotion

    (b) Cold Creams

    (c) Vanishing and Foundation Creams

    (d) Night and Massage Creams

    (e) Hand and Body Creams

    (f) All Purpose Creams

    These are described below :

1. **According to Type of Emulsion Base:**

    (a) Oily Creams: These are w/o emulsions containing lipophilic emulsifying agent such as wool fat/alcohol, divalent soaps, fatty acids etc. These are used as emollient and cleansing agents. Their removal is difficult.

    Example: Cold cream.

(b) **Aqueous Creams:** These are o/w emulsions containing hydrophilic emulsifying agent such as polyethylene glycol, monovalent soaps of fatty acids etc. After application, water from external phase evaporates and leaves cooling sensation on the skin.

   Example: Vanishing cream.

2. **According to their Function:**

   (a) **Cleansing Creams and Lotion:** These are used to remove dirt, oil, grease, sebum, dead cells and crust from the skin.

   (b) **Cold Creams:** These primarily posses an emollient action and are useful for dry skin and quiet popular in winter.

   (c) **Vanishing Creams and Foundation Creams:** These are generally applied to impart fairness to skin and as a component of make-up to hold face powder and improve its adhesion.

   (d) **Night and Massage Creams:** These are used for emollient action. These are applied in night and removed in the morning. They form occlusive layer on the skin and prevents epidermal water loss.

   (e) **Hand and Body Creams:** These are used to maintain moisture to maintain normal skin soft and flexible.

   (f) **All Purpose Creams:** These are specialised creams used to fulfill many functions. These are some what oily but non-greasy.

4.8.2 Formulation of Creams

Drug:

   Drug is dissolved or emulsified in either oil or water according to its solubility.

Bases:

   As creams are emulsions, emulsion bases are mainly used to formulate creams. Absorption bases and water soluble bases are also used in the formulation.

Emulsifier:

   Semisolid emulsions usually require to be stabilised with more than one emulsifier.

   Anionic emulsifier: Alkyl sulphate, amine soaps such as triethanolamine stearates.

   Cationic emulsifier: Quaternary ammonium compounds.

   Non-ionic Emulsifier: Glycol, Glycerol esters, macrogol esters and ethers.

Preservatives:

   Water present in creams promotes microbial growth. To preserve formulation from attack of bacteria and fungi, preservatives are added.

   Examples: Methyl paraben, propyl paraben, benzolkonium chloride, phenyl mercuric nitrate etc.

Benzoic acid is a good antifungal and antibacterial preservative, provided the pH does not exceed 5. It is used in concentration of 0.1% w/v with chloroform to preserve liquid paraffin emulsion B.P.C.

Cetrimide and other quaternary ammonium compounds are occasionally used, in concentration ranging from 0.002 to 0.01 %, to preserve emulsified products for external use. They are bactericidal and effective to vegetative forms of gram-positive organisms, much less effective against gram-negative species, particularly Pseudomonas aeruginosa.

To preserve emulsified preparations containing non-ionic emulgents, the phenylmercuric nitrate and acetate are sometimes employed. They are used in concentrations of 0.004 to 0.01 %.

4.8.3 Manufacturing of Creams

The cream is a semisolid emulsion, consist of oil phase, aqueous phase and emulsifying agent.

1. Creams are prepared by fusion method.

2. Solid waxes are grated and melted on waterbath, high melting materials should be melted first.

3. Strain the molten mass through the nylon cloth to remove foreign matter.

4. Then water soluble ingredients are mixed together, the drug is mixed according to its solubility.

5. During mixing, inner phase is added to the outer phase very slowly.

6. Now, mix with heating oil phase i.e. waxes, oils and other oil soluble ingredients and aqueous phase i.e. water and water soluble ingredients, in a vessel in the presence of emulsifying agent at 75°C with continuous stiring.

7. In aqueous phase 3-5 % excess of water is used to compensate the losses due to evaporation.

8. Flow rate, stirring time and cooling time are important parameters, as these factors decide viscosity, consistency and stability of the product.

9. Perfumes are added at 40-45 °C temperature.

10. Oily perfumes can be easily added to w/o emulsion creams than o/w.

11. Wide range of equipments such as Jacketed kettles, mixers, mills, homogenizers, vacuum pumps are required.

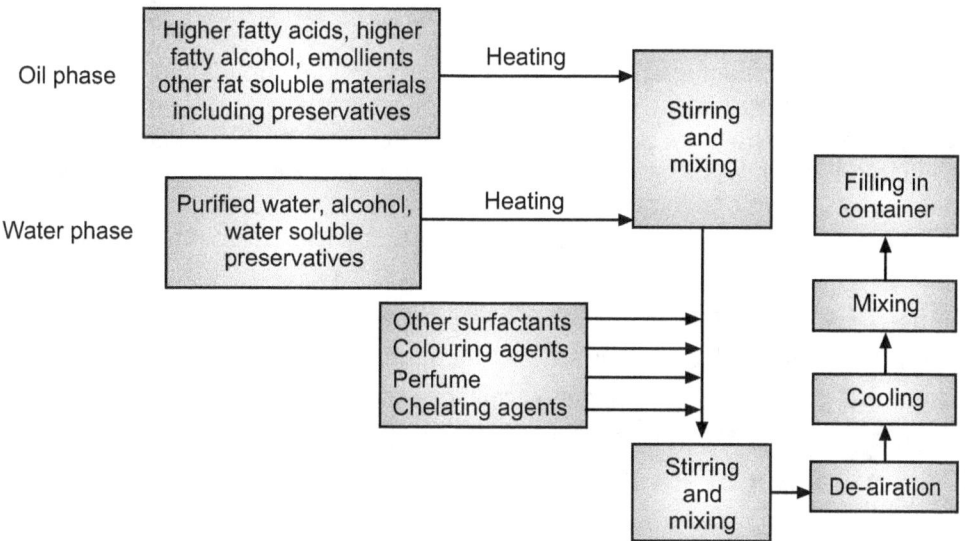

Fig. 4.2: Flow diagram of manufacturing of creams and lotions

Example 1: Cetrimide Cream BPC

Formula:

Cetrimide	0.5 gm
Cetostearyl alcohol	5.0 gm
Liquid paraffin	50.0 gm
Purified water	44.5 gm
Freshly boiled and cooled	

Procedure:

Cetrimide (cationic surfactant) is used in seborrhoea, acne vulgaris, burns and in wounds. It is also a cationic hydrophilic emulsifying agent. Cetostearyl alcohol is non-ionic hydrophobic agent which increases viscosity and improves emollient effect.

1. Prepare aqueous phase by dissolving cetrimide in water and keep it warm.
2. Prepare oily phase by melting cetostearyl alcohol and liquid paraffin and keep it warm.
3. Add aqueous phase in oily phase under constant stirring.
4. Cool the cream and homogenise it.
5. Transfer cream to a suitable wide mouth air-tight container, label and dispense.
6. Label as - FOR EXTERNAL USE ONLY,

   DO NOT FREEZE,

   STORE IN COOL AND DRY PLACE,

   REPALCE CAP TIGHTLY AFTER USE,

   APPLY TO THE AFFECTED AREA.

4.9 Pastes

Pastes, generally contain a large amount (20-50%) of finely powdered solids. So they are often stiffer, more absorptive and less greasy than ointments.

When applied to the skin pastes adhere well, forming a thick coating, protects and soothes inflamed and raw surfaces and minimizes the damage done by scratching in itchy conditions such as chronic eczema.

Due to the powder contents pastes are porous; hence, perspiration can escape and produce protective barrier on the skin.

4.9.1 Types of Pastes

According to hydrophilcity, pastes are classified into following two groups:

(a) Aqueous pastes: E.g. Caboxymethylcellulose sodium paste.

(b) Non-aqueous/Fatty pastes: Compound zinc paste.

4.9.2 Formulation of Pastes

Drug:

The Drug is mostly insoluble and it is passed through sieve no. 85 before formulation.

Bases:

1. **Hydrocarbon base:** Soft paraffin and liquid paraffin are commonly used bases for the preparation of paste.

    Soft paraffin is used as base in Compound Zinc Paste B.P., Compound Zinc and Salicylic acid Paste B.P. (Lassar's Paste), Dithranol paste compound which is used against Eczema, psoriasis.

2. **Water miscible base:** Emulsifying ointment is used as base in Resorcinol and sulfur Paste B.P.C. which is used against Dandruff, and is easily removable from the hair.

3. **Water soluble bases:** Water soluble bases are prepared from mixtures of high and low molecular weight polyethylene glycols (or macrogols). Water soluble dental pastes are used for sterilizing infected root canal.

Thickening Agents:

These are added to maintain the liquid and solid constituents in the form of smooth paste. CMC, methyl cellulose, tragacanth, gum karaya, sodium alginate are used for this purpose.

Humactants:

It will keep the formulation moist. Glycerine, sorbitol and propylene glycol are used.

Surfactants:

Generally, dioctyl sodium sulphosuccinate, sodium lauryl sulphate etc. are used.

Preservatives:

The moisture in paste promotes bacterial growth hence, methyl paraben and propyl paraben are used to preserve the quality of the preparation.

Sweetening Agents:

Sweetners such as saccharine (0.005 - 0.25 %) is added to give sweet taste to oral pastes.

Flavouring Agents:

Peppermint, wintergreen added to impart flavour to the prepearation.

4.9.3 Methods of Preparation of Pastes

Like ointment, pastes are prepared by trituration and fusion methods.

Trituration method is used when the base is liquid or semisolid, an ointment spatula and tile can be used to mix the drug and other ingredients into the base.

Fusion method is used when the base is semisolid and/or solid in nature, in which the base is melted. Then drug and other ingredients are incorporated into it.

Example 1: Compound Zinc Paste

Formula:

Zinc oxide, finely sifted	25 gm
Starch, finely sifted	25 gm
White soft paraffin	50 gm

Type of preparation: Paste with semi-solid base prepared by fusion and trituration.

Procedure:

Zinc oxide is protective, antiseptic and astringent; White soft paraffin is oleaginous base and starch is added to impart the body to the formulation it is absorptive as well.

1. Pass zinc oxide and starch powder through sieve No. 180.
2. Then melt soft paraffin on a water bath.
3. The required amount of powder is taken in a warm mortar, triturated with little melted base until smooth. Gradually rest of the base is added and mixed until cold.
4. Transfer paste to a suitable air-tight container, label and dispense.
5. Label as - FOR EXTERNAL USE ONLY,

   DO NOT FREEZE,

   REPALCE CAP TIGHTLY AFTER USE,

   APPLY TO THE AFFECTED AREA.

Example 2: Coal tar Paste B.P.C.

Formula:

Strong Coal Tar solution B.P.	75 gm
Compound Zinc paste B.P.	925 gm

Type of preparation: Paste with semi-solid base prepared by Trituration.

Procedure:

1. Coal tar is used in psoriasis. Strong coal tar solution is mixed with compound zinc paste.
2. Transfer paste to a suitable air-tight container, label and dispense.
3. Label as - FOR EXTERNAL USE ONLY,

   DO NOT FREEZE,

   REPALCE CAP TIGHTLY AFTER USE,

   APPLY TO THE AFFECTED AREA.

4.10 Jellies

Definition:

Jellies are transparent or translucent, non-greasy, semisolid preparation prepared by using gelling agents and generally applied externally.

They are used for medication, lubrication and some miscellaneous applications. Gelling agents are hydrocolloid substances which gives thixotrophic consistency to the gel. Gelling agents are also known as solidifiers or stabilizers and thickening agents. Gelling agents are more soluble in cold water than hot water.

4.10.1 Types of Jellies

Medicated jellies: It contains considerable amount of water hence water soluble drugs like local anesthetics, spermicides and antiseptics are suitable for incorporation in the gels.

They are easy to apply and evaporation of the water content produces a pleasant cooling effect. The medicinal film usually adheres well and gives protection but is easily removed by washing when the treatment is complete.

e.g. Ephedrine sulfate jelly - Vasoconstrictor used to arrest bleeding from nose.

Pramoxine HCl, a local anesthetic - relieves discomfort of pruritis and hemorrhoids.

Phenyl mercuric nitrate - as spermicidal contraceptive.

Lubricant jelly: These are water soluble, transparent and smooth. These are required for lubrication of catheters, items of eletrodiagnostic equipment, such as cystoscopes, and rubber gloves or finger stalls used for rectal and other examinations. The lubricants must be sterile for articles inserted into sterile regions of the body, such as urinary bladder. For painful investigations a local anaesthetic may be included in the formulation.

e.g. Lignocaine Gel B.P.C.

Miscellaneous Uses:

The following are more specialized jellies –

(a) **Patch testing:** In patch testing, the jelly is the vehicle for allergens applied to the skin to detect sensitivity.

(b) **Electrocardiography:** An electrode jelly may be applied to reduce electrical resistance between the patient's skin and electrodes of the cardiograph. This jelly contains NaCl for providing good conductivity and often pumice powder to remove the horny layer of the epidermis which is the main layer of electrical resistance.

4.10.2 Formulation of Jellies

Pharmaceutical jellies are usually prepared by adding various thickening agents to an aqueous solution, in which drug has been dissolved.

For the preparation of jellies whole gum is preferred rather than powdered gum because the former gives a clear preparation of uniform consistency.

Jelling Agents:

The following gelling agents are used for the preparation of jellies.

1. Tragacanth:

- It is the sap of legumes of several species of genus Astralagus plant.
- It is viscous, odourless and tasteless.
- The 5% concentration of tragacanth is used in medicated gels.
- The 2 - 3% concentration of tragacanth is used in lubricating gels.
- It must be pre-wetted with ethanol or glycerin before dispersion in water to prevent the lump formation.
- Tragacanth acts as demulscent and suspending agent.
- They are susceptible to microbial growth hence requires preservation.

2. Sodium Alginate:

- Algin is water soluble gum.
- It is marketed in the form of sodium, potassium, ammonium alginates.
- **Sodium Alginate:** As lubricant - 1.5 to 2 % is used.
- **Sodium Alginate:** As dermatological vehicle - 5 to 10 % is used.
- The trace of Ca - salt ($CaCl_2$) increase the viscosity.
- It has an advantage over tragacanth that is available in several grades or standardized viscosity.

3. Fenugreek Mucilage:

- Fenugreek mucilage is extracted from multiple maceration of seeds of trigonella foenum graceum.
- It contains polysaccharide.
- It is slowly soluble in cold water but quickly get soluble in hot water and forms viscous colloidal solution.

4. Pectin:

- Pectin is a very good gelling agent for acidic products and is used in the preparation of many types of gels such as edible gels and other gels.
- In dermatological gels, pectin is often used with glycerine and humectants.
- Gels must be packed in well-closed containers because a pectin gel loses water if not stored properly.

5. Starch:

- Starch in combination with gelatin and glycerin is commonly used for preparations of gels.
- Glycerin 50% may act as preservative.
- Medicaments are incorporated in the cold gel by triturating.
- These gels require storage in well closed container to prevent formulation from drying out.

6. Gelatin:

- Gelatin is insoluble in cold water but swell and softens in it.
- It is soluble in hot water.
- Gelatin 15 % gives stiff gellies which are used for protection and support.

7. Cellulose Derivative:

- Methyl cellulose and sodium carboxy methyl cellulose produce neutral,stable, clear with good film strength gels.
- Have good resistance against microbial growth.
- It is clear because they do not contain insoluble impurities.

8. Carbopols:

- Also known as carbomer which is generic name.
- It has high gelling power hence low concentration is sufficient to formulate gelly.
- Carbopols are dry powder with high bulk densities and form acidic aqueous solution of 3.0 pH.
- Carbopols are carboxyvinyl polymers of large molecular weight.

9. Clays:

- Gels containing 7 to 20 % of bentonite can be used as dermatological bases.
- Clays are opalescent and lack attractiveness.
- They are not suitable for application on the skin because of high pH i.e. 9.0.

Preservatives

- As gels contain large quantity of water so preservation is essential.
- It should be compatible with formulation.
- Preservatives such as methyl paraben, propyl paraben are usually used as a preservatives.

4.10.3 Manufacturing of Jellies

- The gelling agents are dissolved either in the aqueous medium or according to their solubility in perticular miscible solvent.
- Mix it properly and allow forming a gel.
- Natural gums require 24 hrs and cellulose polymers requires 48 hrs for complete hydration.
- Gelling can be enhanced by warming aqueous solution such as gelatine, but hot water is not advisable for methyl cellulose dispersion because it requires cold water for gelling.
- Gelling can also be enhanced by keeping the solution overnight for complete salvation of polymer.
- pH of the solution should be maintained, which is an important factor in forming the gel. Sodium alginate, HPMC gels are at pH range 4-10.
- De-aerators are used to remove the problem of bubbles in gels i.e. air entrapment.

Example 1: Zinc-gelatin jelly

Formula:

Zinc oxide	15 g
Gelatin	15 g
Glycerin	35 g
Water	35 g

Procedure:

In this, zinc oxide is protective, antiseptic and astringent, gelatin is gelling agent, glycerine is added to prevent lump formation as it is humectant and water is vehicle.

1. Pass zinc oxide through sieve no. 120.
2. Cut the gelatin and soak gelatin in water until softened.
3. Add glycerin in gelatine solution and heat in water bath. It is heated over bath until the gelatin is dissolved.
4. Required amount of zinc oxide is added in small amounts to the molten base with gentle stirring. Stirring is continued until a viscous product is obtained.
5. Spread the product in tray to a depth of about 1 cm with continuous trituration throughout the operation. When the mass is set carefully, the mass is cut into pieces of about 1.5 cm^2 with a blade or sharp knife.
6. Transfer the gelly to wide mouth, clear glass container, label and dispense.
7. Label as - FOR EXTERNAL USE ONLY,
    DO NOT FREEZE,
    REPALCE CAP TIGHTLY AFTER USE.

4.10.4 Preservation of Jellies

All the jellies contains large quantity of water and they are very prone to microbial growth hence required to be preserved suitably. Bases like clays and cellulose derivative(s) resist microbial contamination. So preservative like Methyl paraben 0.1 to 0.2 % is commonly used.

Bases and medicaments sensitive to heavy metals are sometimes protected by a chelating agent e.g. ethylene diamine tetra acetic acid (EDTA).

4.11 Evaluation Parameters

1. **Appearance:**
    *   Organoleptic properties such as colour and odour of semisolid formulations are evaluated using sensory organs.
    *   Similarly smoothness, homogeneity is also checked by rubbing the product between the fingers.

2. **Particle size:**
    *   Particle size is determined by microscopic study of the particles.

3. **pH:**
    *   pH is an important physical parameter and fluctuation in pH is not desirable as some drugs shows maximum stability at a specific pH value.
    *   The measurement of the pH value provides good control over the manufacturing process and shelf life of the product.
    *   The pH of semisolid formulations is determined by using digital pH meter.
    *   The values should be taken in triplicate and then average values are calculated.

4. **Spreadability:**
   - Semisolids should have good spreadability in order to make application easy. Spreadability test is performed to determine extent of spread ability of semisolids based upon their rheological properties.
   - It is given in terms of time in second taken by two slides to slip off from the formulation under the direction of certain load. Formulation with better spreadability requires less time to separate the two slides.

5. **Penetration:**
   - A weighed quantity of ointment is applied on skin with rubbing on definite area of the skin for given length of time, then collect and weigh the formulation from skin which remains unabsorbed.
   - The difference between two weights can roughly give the idea about the amount of formulation absorbed.

6. **Drug content:**
   - The drug content can be determined using suitable analytical method and result should fall within specified limits.

7. **Viscosity:**
   - The viscosity of the preparation can be measured by using viscometer such as cone and plate viscometer or cup and bob viscometer.
   - The viscosity of the preparation should be such that the product can be easily removed from the container and easily applied to the skin.

8. **Rate of drug release:**
   - Following methods are used to study the rate of release of drug from the formulation.

   Method 1: A clean test tube is taken, of which the internal surface is coated/smeared with the formulation as a thin layer.

   Then pour saline or serum into the test tube. After a certain period of time, the saline or serum is analyzed for the quantity of the drug released. The amount of drug when divided by the time period gives the rate of drug release.

   Method 2: Fill the jar with formulation and close the mouth with cellophane membrane and suspend the jar in water, the amount of drug diffusing in water is then calculated.

   Method 3: Place the formulation on the surface of nutrient agar contained in a petridish which is already been seeded with micro-organism *S. aureus*. After suitable period of incubation a zone of inhibition is measured and it is correlated with the rate of release.

9. **Rate of absorption:**
   - For this test, the ointment should be applied over a definite area of the skin by rubbing.
   - At regular intervals of time, serum and urine samples should be analyzed for the quantity of drug absorbed.
   - The rate of absorption i.e., the amount of drug absorbed per unit time should be more. Diadermic ointment goes deeper into skin and finally reaches into systemic circulation hence diadermic ointment should be evaluated for the rate of absorption.

10. **Extrudability:**
    - Fill the formulations in the collapsible tubes.
    - The extrudability of the formulation is determined in terms of **weight in grams required to extrude a 0.5 cm ribbon of formulation in 10 second.**

11. **Skin irritation test:**
    - The semisolid formulations should not be irritant to the skin. The bases used in the formulation of semisolids may show irritation or allergic reactions.
    - Non-irritancy of the formulation is evaluated by patch test.
    - The hair from the back area of 4 cm^2 is marked on both the sides of the animals, such as rabbits and guinea pigs which are shaved and are used for the test.
    - One side serves as control while the other side is for test formulation.
    - Formulation is applied to the site for given time duration and the site is observed for any sensitivity reaction.
    - The result is recorded by assigning grades. The grade is recorded on 0-3 scale for no reaction to severe erythema with or without edema.

12. **Diffusion study:**
    - For diffusion study, the Franz diffusion cell is used.
    - The cell has two compartments one is Donor compartment - filled with the formulation to be tested is and another is receptor compartment - filled with solvent.
    - Animal or human cadaver skin or cellophane membrane is placed between these two compartments.
    - The amount of drug passed through membrane from donor compartment is measured at regular interval by analyzing the aliquots of fluid using a suitable analytical method.

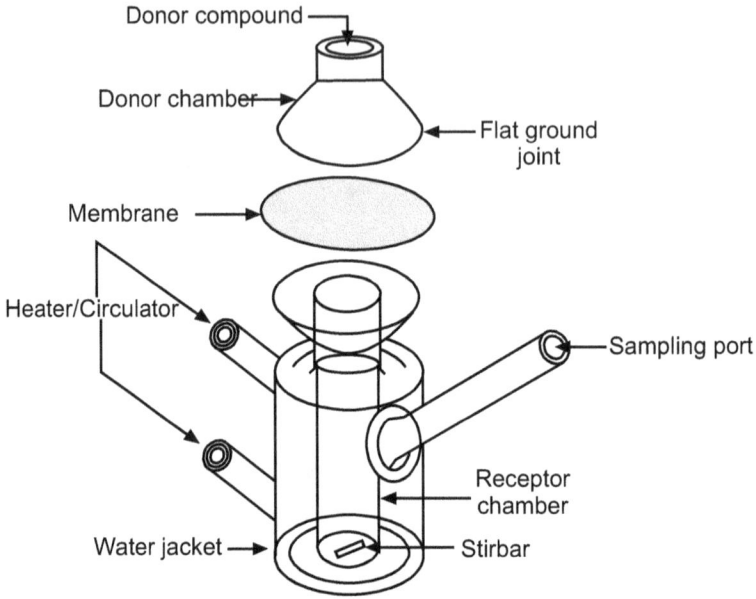

Fig. 4.3: Franz diffusion cell

EXERCISE

1. What are various types of semisolid dosage forms?
2. What are the factors that influence the rate of penetration through the skin?
3. What are penetration enhancers? Give ideal characteristics of penetration enhancers?
4. Explain how the cream can be manufactured.
5. Write in brief the factors governing the selection of ointment bases.
6. Write a short note on Flux.
7. How semisolids are evaluated?
8. Explain the types of bases.
9. Explain the use of different categories of excipients used in a semisolid formulation with suitable example.

✍ ✍ ✍

Chapter ... 5

Manufacturing Equipments

Contents...

5.1 Introduction

The preparation of formulations requires certain amount of energy to mix the ingredients, and additional work must be done to stir the system to overcome the resistance to flow.

In addition, heat often is supplied to the system to melt waxy solids and/or reduce the viscosity of the oil phase and to emulsify the two liquids.

A wide range of equipments are available to fulfill the requirements of the formulation. Equipments should be selected on the basis of production volume and the properties of excipients.

Various types of equipments required for the formulation of Suspensions, Emulsions and Semisolids are described in this chapter.

Some of the factors to be considered to choose the equipment from the wide variety of equipments available are:

•   The quantity of formulation to be prepared.

•   Whether the processing is batchwise or a continuous operation.

•   The rheological characteristics of the final product.

•   The need to incorporate ingredients such as powders or other additives.

•   The operation temperature.

5.2 Equipments for Suspensions, Emulsions and Semisolids

1. **Mortar and Pestle: (For *suspensions, emulsions and semisolids*)**

It is a device used since ancient times, to prepare **suspensions, emulsions and semisolids** and to crush and grind the ingredients into fine powder and paste.

'Mortar' is a bowl made up of ceramic, stone or glass, and 'Pestle' is club shaped object used for crushing and grinding.

The substance to be ground is placed in the mortar and crushed or mixed by using pestle.

Advantages:

1. It is useful for laboratory scale.
2. Small quantity suspensions and emulsions can be prepared in the laboratory.
3. Low cost and easy availability.
4. Its operation is simple.

Disadvantages:

1. Generally, the particle size produced in final product is considerably larger than in other equipments.
2. Not suitable for large scale production.

Fig. 5.1: Mortar and Pestle

2. **Agitators/Mechanical Stirrers: (For *Emulsions*)**

This device is used to prepare **Emulsions.**

Mechanical stirrers are shafts, fitted with impellers, propellers (axial movements) and turbines (radial and tangential movements) which are used to stir the emulsions by placing directly into the formulation. Propeller type stirrers are used for low viscosity emulsions and turbine type stirrers are used for high viscosity emulsions.

The rotational speed of impellers controls the degree of agitation where efficiency of mixing is controlled by type of impeller, its position in the container and general shape of container.

Advantages:

1. These stirrers are used for emulsification of easily dispersed, low-viscosity oils.
2. It is used for small-scale production and laboratory purpose.

Disadvantages:

1. Sometimes it may produce foam and there is also a risk of entrapment of air.
2. Continuous shaking tends to break up the emulsion.

Fig. 5.2: Mechanical stirrer

3. Colloid Mill: *(For Suspension and Emulsion)*

Colloid mill is used for the preparation of suspension and emulsion. Milling occurs when material is passed through the narrow gap between rotor and stator due to shearing.

Colloid mill consist of main three parts that are Hopper, Stator and Rotor. The 'Hopper' is for feeding the material, whereas 'Stator' and 'Rotor' are for producing the shearing action on material fed in the gap between them. Stator is stationary and Rotor is rotating.

The rotor rotates at a speed of 3,000 to 20,000 r.p.m. The stator has milling surfaces and it is steady. The clearance (gap) between the rotor and the stator is adjustable; it is usually from 0.002 to 0.03 inches.

Size reduction is possible due to tremendous shearing of material into narrow gap between rotor and stator which effects a fine dispersion of uniform size.

The suspension or emulsion is fed through the hopper of the mill, which then passes through the narrow gap between rotor and stator and results into fine particle size.

The shearing forces applied in the colloid mill usually increases the temperature within the formulation. Hence, a coolant is used to absorb the excess heat.

Advantage:

1. The main use of a colloid mill is the dispersion of solid particles within a liquid.
2. It has excellent grinding property.
3. It is frequently used to increase the stability of suspensions and emulsions.
4. Colloid mill produces very fine particles in microns.
5. Useful for pharmaceutical suspensions containing poorly wetted solids and viscous emulsions.
6. It has low noise levels.

Disadvantages:

1. It increases the temperature of system and may affect the properties of formulation.
2. It consumes more energy as requires high power for the running of the colloidal mill.

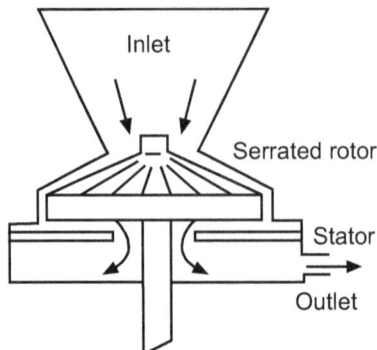

Fig. 5.3: Colloid mill

4. Homogenizers: *(For Suspension and Emulsion)*

Homogenizers are the type of equipments frequently used to produce a satisfactory ***Emulsion and Suspension***. In homogenization, the large globules are converted into small globules.

Homogenization is the process wherein a coarse emulsion is prepared in some other way and is then passed through a narrow orifice under pressure to produce the final product of small particle size with greater degree of uniformity and stability.

Types of Homogenizers:

(1) Hand Homogenizer: Hand homogenizer is a hand pumped machine used to prepare the fine emulsions and suspensions from a coarse one by converting the large globules to small globules by passing through narrow orifice.

Hand homogenizers of the classical type are widely used for manual sample preparation. It is a simple model suitable for the laboratory work for small scale homogenisation of emulsions and suspension.

It consists of a hopper, from which, the material is introduced into the homogeniser which consist of a fine orifice.

It is fitted with a handle which moves up and down and causes coarse emulsion to draw in, through the movement, the emulsion is forced to pass through the fine orifice. The large globules are broken into fine globules of uniform size.

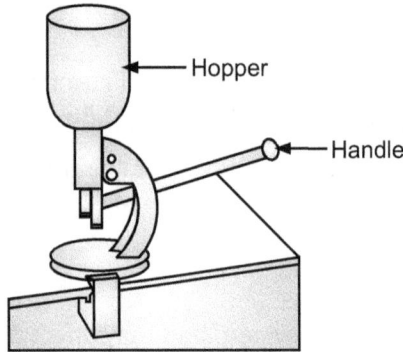

Fig. 5.4: Hand homogenizer

Advantages:

- It is inexpensive.
- It is useful for small-scale extemporaneous preparation of emulsions and suspensions.
- *Hand homogenizer* passes the sample through 10-20 times until a fine homogenate is obtained.

Disadvantages:

- Not suitable for large scale production.

(2) Silverson Mixer Homogenizer: The sliverson homogenizer works on the principle that the large globules in a coarse emulsion are broken into smaller globule by passing them under pressure through a narrow orifice.

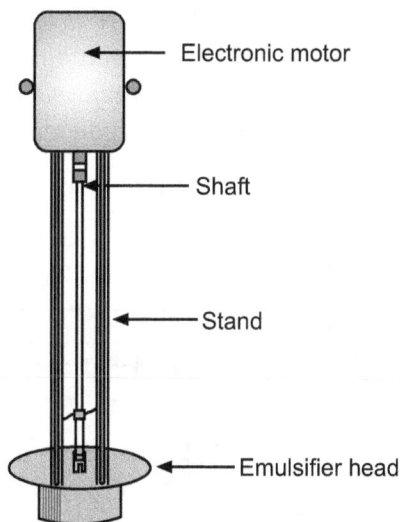

Electronic motor

Shaft

Stand

Emulsifier head

Fig. 5.5: Silverson mixer homogenizer

Silverson mixer homogenisers are the devices which are used to mix or homogenise the coarse particles in the emulsion and suspension to the fine form of reduced particles.

It consist of emulsifier head with number of blades, emulsifier head is covered with a fine meshed stainless steel sieves.

An electric motor fitted at the top rotates these blades at very high speed to produce shearing action.

The emulsifier head is placed in the vessel containing immiscible liquids. The head should be dipped into the immiscible liquids. Motor is started which rotates the blades to produce shearing action and sucks the liquid through the fine holes of stainless steel sieves. Due to this, oil is reduced into small globules.

The Silverson is the high shear laboratory mixing equipment.

Advantages:

1. It is economic and efficient method in producing emulsions typically in the range of 0.5 to 5 microns.
2. It is used for milling both solid and semi-solid materials into either solution or fine suspension.
3. It produces a homogeneous product rapidly and reduces mixing time.

Disadvantages:

1. Shearing force is high and uses high power.

5. Ultrasonic Devices: *(For Emulsions)*

The preparation of **emulsions** by the use of ultrasonic vibrations is also possible. Piezo-electric or magneto restrictive transducers generate sound waves with frequencies > 20 kHz.

Associated pressure gradients cause deformation of droplets.

The quartz plate and electrodes are immersed in an oil bath and, when the oscillator is operating, high-frequency waves flow through the fluid. Emulsification is accomplished by simply immersing a tube containing the emulsion ingredients into this oil bath.

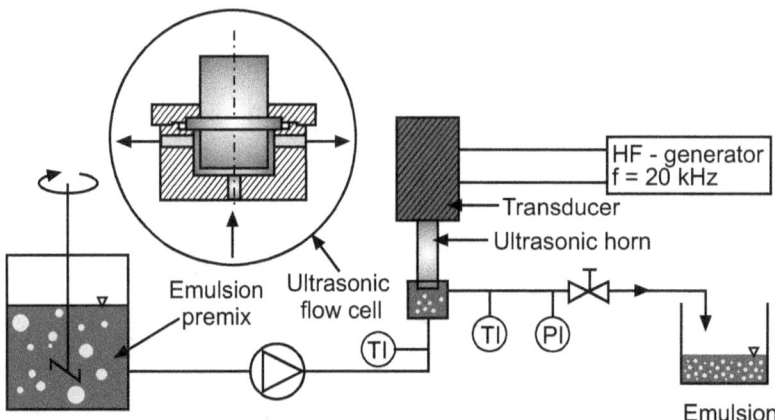

Fig. 5.6: Ultrasonic homogenisation process

Advantages:

It is used for low viscosity and extremely low particle size.

Disadvantages:

It is only for use in laboratory. Large scale production is not possible.

6. Propeller Mixer: *(For Suspensions)*

It is used for mixing relatively low viscosity dispersions (thicker solutions) and maintaining contents in **suspension**.

It is a device comprising a rotating shaft with propeller blades attached in a vessel.

The propeller mixers are operated at very high speed i.e., upto 8000 r.p.m. due to which mixing takes short time and which also gives a satisfactory flow pattern to the liquid.

Propeller mixers are the most widely used form of mixers for liquids of low viscosity. They are much smaller in diameter than paddle and turbine mixers.

Advantages:

1. It is effective in handling liquids having a low viscosity.
2. These are used when high mixing capacity is needed.

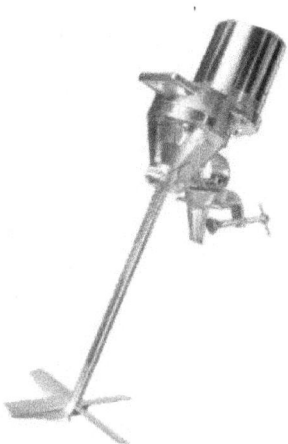

Fig. 5.7: A propeller mixer

Disadvantages:

1. Propellers are not effective with liquids of greater viscosity. For example, glycerin and castor oil.
2. It is not suitable when high shear forces are needed.
3. Vortex formation may happen due to high speed.

Types of Propeller Mixers:

(1) Paddle Mixers: *(For Suspensions)*

Paddle mixers are used in the manufacture of ***Antacid suspensions, Anti-diarroheal mixtures such as bismuth-kaolin mixture.***

Paddle mixers looks like a paddle which consist of flat blades attached to a vertical shaft. This shaft rotates at low speed of 100 r.p.m. or less.

The blades have large surface area which helps them to rotate close to the walls of the container and effectively mix the viscous liquids or semi-solids.

A variety of paddle mixers having different shapes and sizes are used in a pharmaceutical industry, depending on the nature and viscosity of the product.

Advantage:

The paddle mixers have low speed; so vortex formation is not possible which will prevents entrapment of air.

Disadvantage:

Mixing of the suspensions is poor, thus, baffled tanks are required.

(2) Turbine Mixers: *(For Emulsions)*

Turbines give greater shearing forces than propellers and thus they are more suitable for preparation of **emulsions**.

Turbine mixers consist of vessel and a circular disc impeller to which a number of short, straight or curved blades are attached. These mixers are rotated at a lower speed than propellers. The mixer produces greater shear forces than propellers therefore they are used for mixing liquids of high viscosity such as glycerine, liquid paraffins etc. and has a special application in the preparation of emulsions.

Fig. 5.8: Turbine blades

Advantages:

1. Turbines are highly efficient.
2. They can bring rapid blending of low viscosity materials of large volumes producing intense dispersion.

Disadvantages:

1. Vortex formation may occur.

7. Scraped Surface Agitators: *(For Emulsions)*

These agitators are required for **emulsification** where heat transfer is essential. In this, the flexible and movable blades are attached to the anchor which scrapes the side walls of the vessel. Hence, this is known as Scraped Surface Agitators.

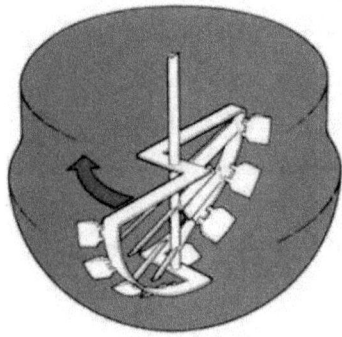

Fig. 5.9: Scraped surface agitators

8. Agitator Mixers: *(For semi-solids)*

Agitator mixers include Sigma mixers and Planetary mixers.

These mixers are designed specifically for **semi-solids**. They are usually of heavier construction to handle materials of greater consistency. The agitator arms are designed in such a way, that, they can perform a pulling and kneading action. The shape and movement of agitator is such that material is cleared from all sides and corners of the mixing vessel.

Types of Agitator Mixer:

(1) Sigma Arm Mixers: This mixer is used for the mixing of semisolids.

It has two blades, shape of which resembles the greek letter "Sigma". The speed of these blades is different and they move towards each other. One blade usually rotates twice the speed of the other.

The blades operate in a mixing vessel which has a double trough shape. Each blade is fitted into a trough. The difference in speed and shape of the blades causes end to end movement.

Entrainment of air is one of the problems encountered in the mixing of semi-solids. Hence, this mixer can be enclosed and operated under reduced pressure, which is an excellent method for avoiding entrainment of air. This may assist in minimizing decomposition of oxidisable materials, but it must be used with caution if volatile ingredients are present in the mix.

Advantages:

1. Sigma blade mixer creates a minimum dead space during mixing.
2. Being of sturdy construction and higher power, this form of mixer can handle even the heaviest plastic materials, and products such as pill masses, tablets granule masses and ointments are mixed readily.

Disadvantage:

1. Sigma mixers work at a fixed speed.
2. Entrapment of air in the mixing of semisolids.

(2) Planetary Mixers: This mixer is used for the mixing of *semisolids*.

Mixing element moves around its own axis and around the central axis like a planet and reach to the every part of the vessel. Hence, this mixer is given a name Planetary Mixer. The blades of a mixer tear the mass apart and shear is applied between a moving blade and a stationary wall. Movement of blades facilitates uniform mixing.

It consists of stationary stainless steel vessel, fitted with mixing blade at the top. The mixing blade is driven by electric motor. There is a narrow clearance between blade and wall of the vessel which provides accurate kneading and shear action required for effective mixing. Initially the speed of the blade is slow and then it increases gradually.

Fig. 5.10 (a): Planetary mixers

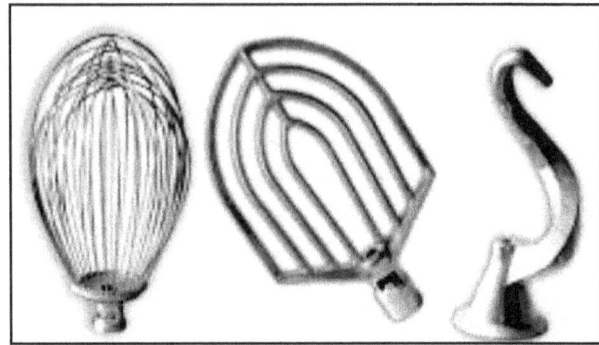

Fig. 5.10 (b): Different blade attachment available for planetary mixer

Advantages:

1. It is used for mixing and blending in pharmaceutical industry.
2. Planetary mixers work at varying speeds.
3. This is more useful for wet granulation and is advantageous over sigma mixers.

Disadvantages:

1. For working, planetary mixers require high power, hence mechanical heat may build up within the powder mix.
2. Its use is limited to batch work only.

9. Triple-Roller Mill: *(For semi-solids)*

Various types of roller mills consisting of one or two or more rollers are commonly used but triple roller mill is preferred. Triple-roller mill is composed of three rollers of a hard abrasion-resistant material.

These rollers are fitted in such a way that they come in close contact with each other and rotated at different rates of speeds. The material which comes in-between the rollers are crushed and reduced in particle size. The reduction in particle size depends on the gap between the rollers and difference in their speeds. The gap between rollers C and D is usually less than the gap between B and C.

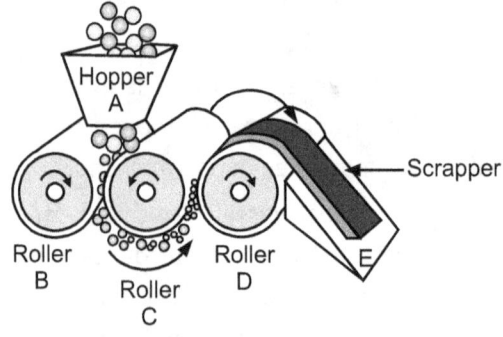

Fig. 5.11: Triple-roller mill

As shown in Fig. 5.11 the material is passed through the hopper A, which then continues to pass through roller between B and C where it is reduced in size. Then this material is again passed between the rollers C and D where it is further reduced in size and a smooth mixture is obtained. After passing the material between rollers C and D, the smoothened and uniform material is continuously removed from roller D by means of scraper E, and then it is collected in a receiver.

Advantages:

1. The triple roller mill is suitable for continuous processes.
2. It is used to obtain an ointment of smooth and uniform texture.
3. It produces very uniform dispersion.

Disadvantages:

1. Roll deflection may occur.
2. It is difficult to maintain a uniform gap between the rolls.
3. There will be little or no effect on fibre materials.

10. Ointment Slab: *(For semi-solids)*

An ointment slab and large metal spatulas can be used for the preparation of ointments. Ointment slabs are either ground glass plates or porcelain and provide a hard, non-absorbable surface for mixing.

When drug is required to be mixed with ointment bases by trituration method, in that case slab and spatula is used.

Spatula is also useful in breaking up of lumps and transfer of ointment into container.

Ointment slabs have the advantage that "clean-up" is quicker. Large metal spatulas are used instead of smaller metal spatulas because they have the proper combination of flexibility and strength for adequate shearing and mixing.

Black rubber or plastic spatulas are not used in ointment compounding.

For preparing a large quantity of ointment, ointment slab and spatula is not preferred. In large scale production, ointment mills and electric mortar and pestle as a mixing device is recommended, which produce very smooth and elegant ointments.

Fig. 5.12: Ointment slab

5.3 Layout and Designing of Manufacturing Facility for Semisolids as Per Schedule M

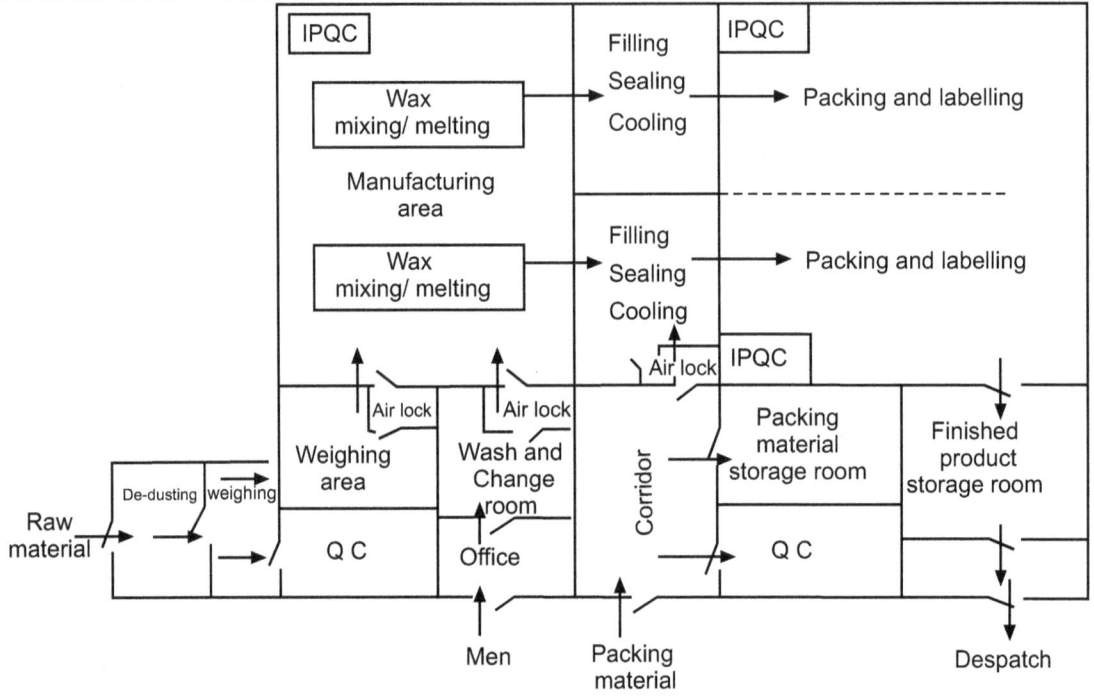

Fig. 5.13: Plant layout for manufacture of semisolids

GMP in Topical Products:

Semisolid dosage forms include creams, ointments, paste and lotions.

The manufacturing facilities for semisolid dosage forms are as follows:

- The entrance to the area where semisolid products are manufactured should be through a suitable airlock. Outside the airlock, insectocutors shall be installed.
- The air to this manufacturing area shall be filtered through at least 20 µ air filters.
- An exhaust system of suitable capacity shall be fitted to effectively remove vapours, fumes, floating dust particles.
- The equipment used shall be designed and maintained to prevent the product from being accidentally contaminated with any foreign matter or lubricant.
- Suitable cleaning equipment and material shall be used in the process of cleaning or drying the process equipment or accessories used.
- No rags or dusters shall be used in the process of cleaning or drying the process equipment.
- Water used in compounding shall be purified water IP.
- Powders whenever used shall be suitably sieved before use.

- Heating vehicles and base like petroleum jelly shall be done in separate mixing area in suitable stainless steel vessels using steam, gas electricity, solar energy etc.
- A separate packaging section may be provided for primary packaging of the products.

A Plant Layout for Semisolid Manufacture shown in Fig. 5.13 has Following Sections:

1. **Raw Material:** Procured material is stored and issued from this section.

2. **De-dusting:** It is carried out to remove dust and other fine impurities from boxes, and containers of raw material.

3. **Wash and Change rooms :** Washing of equipments and changing is done here.

4. **Weighing:** Materials required for the manufacturing of the batch are weighed. Quantity of material to be weighed depends upon the batch size.

5. **Manufacturing:** For manufacturing, the mixing equipments are used. Mixing equipments should effectively move semisolid mass from outside walls to the center and from bottom to top of the kettle. Motor is used to drive mixing system and must be able to handle the product at its most viscous stage.

   Manufacturing essentially includes the melting of bases for which the working temperature range must be ideal with respect to ingredients and type of product. Other parameters like Mixing speed, Shear, Product viscosity are also important.

6. **Filling, Sealing and Cooling:** Semisolids are filled into the container and then sealed. For filling of semisolids various pumps of suitable size and type are used.

   Product compatibility with the Pump surface, Pumping rate, Pumping pressure should essentially be monitored. Product is cooled to set the semisolids.

7. **IPQC:** This section is provided with various equipments essential for the *In process quality control test* of semisolids. IPQC tests are carried out before and after filling of product, in a separate area provided in a layout.

8. **Packing Material Storage Area:** Packing materials such as glass, plastic screw capped jars, metal and plastic collapsible tubes, foils etc. are stored are stored in this area. There is separate entry for packaging material to get in, to avoid cross contamination.

9. **Packing and Labelling:** This area is provided with various equipments of packing and labelling.

10. **Quality Control:** Various quality control tests such as pH, Viscosity, Spreadability, Skin irritation, Drug contents determination, Assay of active ingredients, Uniformity and Homogeneity test, Filling test etc. are carried out in this area. There is separate QC area for raw material testing and finished product testing.

11. **Finished Product Storage Room:** Finished products are stored in this area and after QC clearance then finished product is dispatched.

5.4 Layout and Designing of Manufacturing Facility for Suspension, Emulsion As Per Schedule M

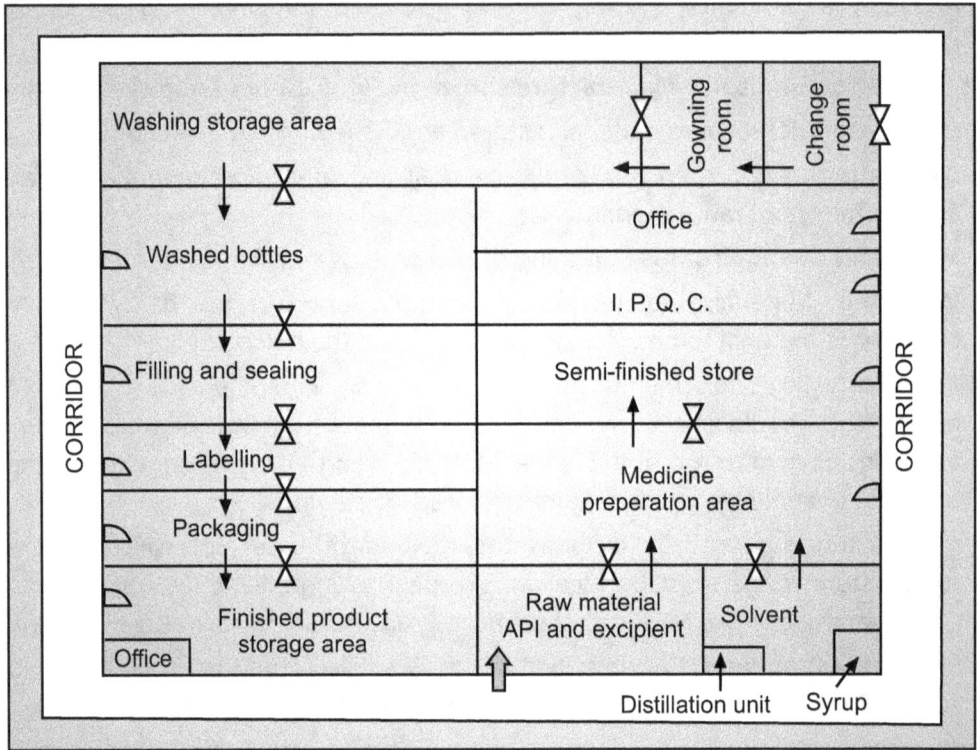

Fig. 5.14: Plant layout for manufacture of suspension and emulsion

GMP in Liquid Orals:

These dosage forms include syrups, elixirs, emulsions and suspensions.

The Manufacturing Facilities for Suspension and Emulsion are as follows:

(i) Building and Equipment:

1. The premises and equipment shall be designed, constructed and maintained to suit the manufacturing of oral liquids. The layout and design of the manufacturing area shall strive to minimize the risk of cross-contamination and mix-ups.

2. Manufacturing area shall have entry through double door air-lock facility. It shall be made fly proof by use of 'fly catcher' and/or 'air curtain'.

3. Drainage shall be of adequate size and have adequate traps, without open channels and the design shall be such as to prevent back flow. Drains shall be shallow to facilitate cleaning and disinfecting.

4. The production area shall be cleaned and sanitized at the end of every production process.

5. Tanks, containers, pipe work and pumps shall be designed and installed so that they can be easily cleaned and sanitized. Equipment design shall be such as to prevent accumulation of residual microbial growth or cross-contamination.

6. Stainless steel or any other appropriate material shall be used for parts of equipments coming in direct contact with the products. The use of glass apparatus shall be minimum.

7. Arrangements for cleaning of containers, closures and droppers shall be made with the help of suitable machines/devices equipped with high pressure air, water and steam jets.

8. The furniture used shall be smooth, washable and made of stainless steel or any other appropriate material which is scratch proof, washable and smooth.

(ii) Purified Water:

1. The chemical and microbiological quality of purified water used shall be specified and monitored routinely. The microbiological evaluation shall include testing for absence of pathogens and shall not exceed 100 cfu/ml (as per Appendix 12.5 of IP 1996).

2. There shall be a written procedure for operation and maintenance of the purified water system. Care shall be taken to avoid the risk of microbial proliferation with appropriate methods like recirculation, use of UV treatment, treatment with heat and sanitizing agent. After any chemical sanitization of the water system, a flushing shall be done to ensure that the sanitizing agent has been effectively removed.

(iii) Manufacturing:

1. Manufacturing personnel should wear wherever required non-fiber shedding clothing to prevent contamination of the product.

2. Materials likely to shed fiber like gunny bags, or wooden pallets shall not be carried into the area where products or cleaned containers are exposed.

3. Care should be taken to maintain the homogenity of emulsion by use of appropriate emulsifier and suspensions by use of appropriate stirrer during filling. Mixing and filling processes shall be specified and monitored. Special care shall be taken at the beginning of the filling process, after stoppage due to any interruption and at the end of the process to ensure that the product is uniformly homogenous during the filling process.

4. The primary packaging area should have an air supply which is filtered through 5 micron filters. The temperature of the area should not exceed 30 °C.

5. When the bulk product is not immediately packed, the maximum period of storage and storage conditions shall be specified in the Master Formula. The maximum period of storage time of a product in the bulk stage shall be validated.

A Plant Layout for Liquid Manufacture shown in Fig. 5.14 **has Following Sections:**

1. **Raw Material**: (API and Excipients) Procured API and Excipients are stored and issued from this section.

2. **Distillation Unit**: Distilled water required for manufacturing is prepared in this unit.

3. **Medicine Preparation Area:**

   Suspension: Dispersions of drugs and excipients in suitable solvent are prepared.

Some parameters are required to be considered while manufacturing, like selection of sieves which should not remove any of the active ingredients, addition and dispersion of suspending agents (Lab scale – sprinkling method and Production scale – vibrating feed system), time and temperature required for hydration of suspending agent, mixing speeds as required but high speed may leads to entrapment of air in the formulation, and selection of the equipment according to the batch size.

Emulsion: Manufacture of emulsion requires consideration of many parameters like- Temperature, Phase volumes, Phase viscosities, Phase densities etc. similarly, selection of type of mixing equipment, homogenizing equipment, In-process or final product filters, screens , pumps and filling equipment, and of course which ultimately depends upon the nature of product and batch size.

4. **Semi-finished store:** This section is meant for the storage of prepared medicaments.

5. **IPQC:** This section is provided with various equipments essential for the *In-process quality control test* of liquids. IPQC tests are carried out before filling the product in container.

6. **Change Room and Gowning Room:** This section is provided to avoid contamination of product from working personnel.

7. **Washing area:** Washing of bottles and equipments is done in this area and then stored in the separate area provided for storage.

8. **Filling, Sealing:** Suspensions and emulsions are filled into glass, plastic screw capped bottles and then sealed. For filling of liquids various pumps of suitable size and type are used.

9. **Packing and Labelling:** This area is provided with various equipments required for packing and labelling.

10. **Finished Product Storage Room:** Finished products are stored in this area, and after QC clearance the finished product is dispatched.

11. **Quality Control:** Various quality control tests such as pH, Viscosity, Drug contents determination, Assay of active ingredients etc. are carried out in this area.

EXERCISE

1. Write short note on manufacturing equipments for preparation of suspension?
2. Explain the different mechanical equipments available for emulsification.
3. Write down briefly about equipments for preparation semisolids.
4. Explain the manufacturing layout of semisolids.

✎ ✎ ✎

www.ingramcontent.com/pod-product-compliance
Lightning Source LLC
Chambersburg PA
CBHW080732020726
47503CB00010B/2883